INTRIGUING ESCAPADE AT SWIM CAMP

By

SHERRY WALRAVEN

© COPYRIGHT 2024 BY SHERRY MOSS WALRAVEN
ISBN: 978-1-963735-30-7 (Paperback)
978-1-963735-31-4 (E-book)

All rights reserved. No part of this book may be reproduced or transmitted in any form or by any means, electronic or mechanical, including photocopying, recording, or by any information storage and retrieval system, without permission in writing from the copyright owner.

The views expressed in this work are solely those of the author and do not necessarily reflect the views of the publisher, and the publisher disclaims any responsibility for them.

To order additional copies of this book, contact:

Proisle Publishing Services LLC
39-67 58th Street, 1st floor
Woodside, NY 11377, USA
Phone: (+1 646-480-0129)
info@proislepublishing.com

Dedicated to my Granddaughter, Michaela.

Thanks for giving me the information

to put in this book.

You are great!

What is Swimming?

Heart pounding

Arms stroking

Legs kicking

Blood pumping

Fingers gliding through the water

Instructor yelling kick kick kick

Eyes locked on the end

Arms splashing

Legs pounding on the water

123 breath 123 breath 123 breath

And that's swimming.

By Jake S.

TABLE OF CONTENTS

Introduction	9
Chapter 1	11
Chapter 2	16
Chapter 3	19
Chapter 4	24
Chapter 5	26
Chapter 6	28
Chapter 7	31
Chapter 8	33
Chapter 9	36
Chapter 10	41
Chapter 11	44
Chapter 12	47
Chapter 13	51
Chapter 14	56
Chapter 15	59
Chapter 16	63
Chapter 17	66
Chapter 18	69

Chapter 19	73
Chapter 20	76
Chapter 21	79
Chapter 22	84
Chapter 23	86
Chapter 24	89
Chapter 25	91
Chapter 26	94
Chapter 27	97
Chapter 28	100
Chapter 29	103
Chapter 30	105
Chapter 31	107
Chapter 32	109
Chapter 33	114
Chapter 34	118
Chapter 35	122
Chapter 36	125
Chapter 37	127
Chapter 38	132

Chapter 39	136
Chapter 40	140
Chapter 41	144
Chapter 42	147
Chapter 43	152
Chapter 44	154
Chapter 45	156
Chapter 46	159
Chapter 47	164
Chapter 48	166
Chapter 49	170
Chapter 50	172
Epilogue	176

INTRODUCTION

The splashing of the swimmers, who came for practice, was giving it all they could as they did the butterfly stroke, backstroke, breaststroke, and ending with twenty minutes of free style. Getting ready for competitions could be strenuous as they went through their routine of different strokes. Swimmers were excited and maybe a touch nervous as they were thinking about the competition, wondering if their time was okay and would Coach Sheila think they were good enough. It could make a swimmer somewhat jittery with anticipation of an upcoming competition.

It took a great amount of energy and a strong desire to do their best to win their heat. The thrill of competition was invigorating as they went through the actions of their stroke. The coach didn't seem to be concerned because they were good swimmers, and she was wanting a championship this year.

One thing no one noticed as the swimmers went through their strokes, was the person watching intensely at them as they did their practice session. This person had memories of wanting to be a good swimmer, but things at home put a stop to the chance of being a competition swimmer. Sometimes things just happen.

The wanna-be swimming champion began thinking, "That should be me in the water going through my stokes instead of these girls, who were good, but I am better. If something was to happen to them, maybe they would let me compete. I know I am a little too old, but hey, I still look young. That is something to think about. I overheard that they were going to a lake to practice for a couple of nights. That might give me a chance to do my thing. I could still be a great swimmer. I guess I will be making a trip to the lake where the swimmers will be. This just might be what I need. Perhaps I could replace one of the girls," thought the one with a huge smile, who wanted to be the champion she thought she could be. She was older and more experienced than these girls. Perhaps one of them will be hurt and can't do their heat. I could jump in her place. That is just what she needs. She did not want anyone to be hurt, but if it was just a little bit, maybe it wouldn't be so bad. She just might be a champion swimmer yet. Everyone would think differently of me if I were a champion. She would like to make her dad and her brothers proud of her. She was the only girl in the family, so she knew they would be proud.

Chapter One

The enflamed sun was making shadows through the large windows of the natatorium where teams of swimmers practiced for an important competition to be held soon. The parents, who were waiting to pick up their son or daughter, could hear the splash of swimmers as they practice, along with whistles blowing, voices of swim coaches, and the strong smell of chlorine filling the air.

"Great job, Grace. Keep up that pace," hollered Coach Sheila, who was Grace's new swim coach this year. All the team liked Coach Sheila and thought she was a fantastic coach, and she could be funny sometimes. Some of them wanted to be like her, even though they didn't know her very well. She was new, so they haven't had much time to get to know her well. She seemed nice, but you never know about a person unless you are around them more often. The swimmers thought Coach Sheila would probably be okay. She was fun at times, but somewhat cranky at other times.

Grace Waldon wasn't too sure, at first, if she even wanted to do the swim thing. Coach Sheila could be a harsh taskmaster at times, but Grace realized that Coach could also make it fun, and she liked fun and being here with her friends, so she decided to keep up what she began three years ago. Her friends would be disappointed if she had dropped out, because they all wanted to be together, and this was a good time to do that. The girls were more like sisters than just friends, and that was the way they liked it.

The Gillygut twins, Silver and Gold, along with Lisa Acre were all best friends with Grace, and they were all on the same swim team. When you saw one, you saw them all. They had been best friends since first grade and here they were already in the ninth grade now. They were the coaches' best swimmers, or so Coach Sheila told them, but she may tell all the swimmers that so they will do well to make her proud. Coach Sheila was a hard person to figure out what she was thinking at any given moment.

Grace's parents had a conversation with her and explained that sometimes coaches get a bit excited and that doesn't mean they are a bad person. It means they are a good coach, who cares for their swimmers. They told Grace she did not need to quit what she started. Grace smiled because she loved her parents and wanted to do what they said. Much to Grace's dismay, they were usually right.

After practice, Coach Sheila had a meeting with the swimmers and their parents to see how well her idea will be received. She didn't know how well the parents would take her idea. They may not like it, and that is entirely possible they won't like it. It would require taking their kids away from home for a few days. Of course, she would have to recruit some other coaches to help her with the practice sessions. They could also double as chaperones.

"It has been brought to my attention, there is a lake in the next county where swimmers can hone their swimming skills. The lake is not very deep, and I would like for my team to stay several days and practice. It would not cost the parents anything, because we will be staying in a bunkhouse requiring each swimmer to have a sleeping bag, or some linens. I will be providing the meals for the trip," explained the smiling coach. She knew she needed to play nice with the parents, because she needed to have them on her side.

"I have something else I know the parents would like to know. I have confiscated some more swimming coaches to be chaperones and will help with the drills we will be doing. All the coaches will be in the water while the swimmers are practicing, so they will not be in the water alone." Coach Sheila was hoping for the best. She knew parents were cautious with their children.

One of the parents asked, "How about restroom facilities?" Coach knew the parents would be concerned about details, and she would make sure she said everything just right. There would be no room for mistakes on her part. She had some trouble in her other school, so she needed to be careful.

"Good question," said Coach Sheila. "It's a large bunkhouse where we will be staying with a large room with bunk beds, a large kitchen, and a large restroom with showers. I will take the food, and a first aid kit. The owners put a chemical around the lake that keeps the snakes from entering the water. They have never had a problem with any other swim teams before. It should be a productive camp to practice for our competition, and I hope you will trust us with your swimmers."

Coach Sheila smiled at the crowd and began introducing the other adults, who will be helping her. "These are my helpers, who are all championship swimmers. Beginning on the right of the row is Dan, Hally, Bell, Jaybird, Hank, and Maggie. Do not worry, parents. They are professionals, and we all will be working together to train and take care of your swimmers. It should be good for the competition to have this training."

After Coach Sheila's speech, all parents signed the permission slip except for one, whose parents were taking their family to see Mount Rushmore. Coach was happy and could not wait to begin the swim camp with her "Platinum Winners."

The swimmers were excited about pursuing this adventure. Grace, Silver, Gold, and Lisa couldn't wait to spend three days together. They knew they wouldn't swim all day, so perhaps they would have time to explore what else that might be here around the lake. They were hoping there was a zipline. The girls knew they would have fun even if there wasn't anything else there at the camp.

CHAPTER TWO

Coach Sheila had high hopes for her girls this year. She could feel in her bones that she had her championship team. She thought she did last year, at a different school, but the girls let her down. She had high hopes for this team. Changing schools may be the best decision she had ever made. She felt this would be her chance for having a championship team, and that is why she even does this. She gets a championship team, and then she quits for good. She really didn't like kids, but she would put up with them to get her championship. She sure didn't like the notion of the parents finding out she didn't like kids. She would lose her job, for sure.

Sheila Brown liked her girls a little bit that she coached. They knew if they had a problem, she was always there for them, or at least, that is what she tells them. She didn't need any teenager problems to deal with. She had been coaching swim teams for fifteen years, and she loved every minute of it. She was hoping for that championship this year. She had great swimmers, who could do great under pressure. Most of the girls were close friends which gave them incentive to do their best. It was like, at times, the girls were going against each other. It didn't bother her, because it gave the girls incentive.

She knew she sometimes could get somewhat testy with her girls, but she remembers her dad being harsh with her. She wanted to forget the beatings he doled out to her and her brothers, which was often. One of her brothers had to be taken to the hospital with a broken arm after one of her dad's beatings. She often wondered if their dad loved anyone, especially his kids. Their mom ran away when Sheila was only twelve, because she didn't want to put up with their dad. Her brothers were older than her, so they raised each other.

Sheila contributes all her problems in her past due to her dear ole dad. She had a tendency, at times, to lose control, and that wasn't good in her line of work. This very thing has been her downfall a couple of times in the past. Yeah, she hit one of her swimmers, who she said was the reason they lost the championship. Before she was at that school, she had an incident where she lost her temper and broke the hand of a girl who simply just asked her a question. Coach told the girl she had already given her instructions, and she should have listened the first time. Sheila thought she may have been a bit too harsh, but that's all she knew to do, because that is the way her dear ole dad did it. You had to listen or pay the consequences.

"Were you not listening when I gave the instructions, you little brat?" asked Coach Sheila with a scowl on her face. Parents took offense to her tactics and got her fired from one of the schools where she was before now. Well, if she was being honest with herself, she had been fired from every school she was ever worked, but these parents, and the school principal didn't need to know what she did before she came to their school.

The girl began crying right before Sheila, with all her strength, pushed the girl into a block wall. Of course, she lost her job. She did not leave those schools on her own. She was fired from both schools. She lucked up with this job, and she didn't want to lose it. She was trying her best to not lose control. Her therapist was always on-call for her. She sure didn't want to be fired again, because no other school would hire her. She didn't know what she would do if that happened.

She didn't need for the parents of her girls to find out about her past. That wouldn't be good at all. Sheila did not need to get another job. She would pray the parents never found out her past, because if they did, she knew they would have her fired, and she sure didn't want that to happen. If they found out, it would be her undoing. She would never be the same again. Just a woman without a job and nothing to do with her time. She didn't think anyone could find out about her past anyway, so she wouldn't worry about it. Worrying didn't solve problems or make them go away.

CHAPTER THREE

The big day finally arrived to go to their first-ever swim camp. They didn't know everything that would take place, but it had to be great in the minds of the group of best friends. The girls all met at Grace's house. Everyone had already gotten to Grace's house except Lisa. Her parents were out of town, so the maid would be bringing her here any minute now. The girls were ready for this camp. They were going to have so much fun, and they couldn't wait for it to happen.

The girls began to giggle as they saw Lisa get out of her maid's car. The maid's car was tiny with rust on both bumpers, and the doors squeaked while the engine backfired every five minutes. Lisa ran up to the others, because she was so happy to be going to swim camp with her friends. She needed to be with them and have some fun. It gets her mind off her parents not caring about her. She missed her parents. They weren't always gone all the time when she was little, but the older she became, the more they stayed away. They must have thought the maid could raise her. Lisa loved her maid, because she seemed to really care about her, and wanted what was best for her. She would always take up for me when her parents were home and saw something they didn't like.

"Okay, little ladies. Look and see if you have everything on the list. You don't want to leave anything," said Grace's mom who was checking everything out for the girls. Everybody gave her a thumbs-up telling her they had everything they needed.

They all piled into Grace's mom's car, so she could take them to the school where the bus was that will take them to swim camp. The bus was filled with giggling teenagers who couldn't wait to see what was in store for them at this camp. They knew they would have fun but didn't know if there was anything else to do on their off time. They figured they would just have to wait and see when they arrived. They may have time when they first arrive to check out everything around the camp.

The bus finally made it to the lake beside a huge building. Girls and boys made it off the bus. The boys began unloading the luggage from underneath the bus, while the girls picked up their luggage and headed for the girls' bunkhouse. All the boys could hear was the girl's loud giggles. They couldn't understand why girls like to giggle, but all the girls they knew giggled, and sometimes for no reason at all. The boys thought girls were strange.

"Ladies and gentlemen," hollered Coach in a loud voice, so all could hear over the din of the excited teenage voices. "Go get your luggage and put it in the bunkhouse. We will meet in thirty minutes for our first swim practice. Don't be late. If you are late, you miss dinner, so if you want to eat, you won't be late." Coach Sheila didn't put up with being tardy, or most anything else either.

After the allotted time, the girls went to the lake where the adults were gathered to help the teenagers get in some practice. It was different than the pool, but they got used to it in no time at all. After a couple of hours, the girls went back to the bunkhouse to put on dry clothes and decided to go exploring to see what they could find. Coach shouldn't mind, because they were going to get lots of exercise in while they searched. They decided the more they walk, the more exercise they would get.

They searched and searched and found a zipline at the park, which was good. They walked a little farther and found a big cave. They stood staring at the opening of the cave wondering if they should go inside it, or not. None of them had ever been inside a cave before making them want to go inside this one just to see what one looked like. On the outside looking at the dark entry to the cave made the girls sort of jumpy.

"Wow! We need to see what's in there," said Silver in a rousing voice. She has always been on the audacious side of life. Sometimes when she wants to do something, she runs right in and the others have to follow to make sure she doesn't do something dopey.

"I guess we could go in just a little way," said a cautious Grace, who really didn't want to go, but she would go with her friends. After all, how bad could it be.

Not even one of these ladies had ever been in a cave before, so they thought it wouldn't hurt to see what's in a dark cave. Hopefully, it wasn't a huge bear, but no one wanted to think about that.

The girls elected Silver to lead the way into the unknown. She took her phone out of her pocket to use the flashlight. Some of the others did the same. They saw a ledge where someone could sit, along with a stream that led into another larger body of water. That might just need to be explored, but not today, because Coach told everyone to meet at the campfire for dinner shortly, and time was about to run out. Perhaps they could go in the cave tomorrow, or another day.

"I am pretty certain we have time to look just a little bit farther and see where this water goes," said Gold who was bold also, but not as much as her twin sister. She would usually do what her sister did, whether she wanted to, or not.

"Maybe this water getting larger might mean this cave goes somewhere else. Wow!" said Lisa, who couldn't believe she was even inside a cave, but she was liking this quest.

"What time is it? We were told not to go far because dinner would be cooked outside, and we will need to cook our own food," said Grace, who thought this cave visit was kind of neat until she heard a noise that didn't sound good. The girls jumped as high as a girl could jump when a raccoon ran toward the entrance of the cave. At least, it wasn't a bear. They all began laughing at the raccoon and were grateful it wasn't something larger.

"I guess that dang ole raccoon didn't like our company," said Silver as she laughed out loud making a small echo in the cave. When the others heard Silver's echo, they all began laughing so they could hear their own echo. That was the coolest thing that had happened today.

"Maybe we should go back to the camp now," smiled Grace. She thought the cave and the raccoon were interesting, and it was definitely worth another visit to the gloomy cave at some point before leaving for home.

The girls didn't know they had been followed by the school bully. He wasn't really a bully, but he liked to play tricks on people. They all turned around and saw Zeke Sheet.

Chapter Four

Zeke Sheet was a bizarre boy. He couldn't be called a bully, because he wasn't mean enough. That didn't stop him from playing pranks on almost everyone. He only did it to people he knew could take it, or if it was someone who he would like for a friend. Not everybody wants a friend who tricks people.

He lived in a small white house with his mom, who has to work long hours to keep them in rent and food money. His dad took off before he was even born. Guess being a dear ole dad wasn't his cup of tea, but him and his mom have a good relationship. He may not wear designer clothes, but that was okay with him. He loved his mom, so all was okay.

His mom scraped up enough money for him to be on the boys' swim team. That was about the only thing he was good at. He did odd jobs for people around his neighborhood to earn his lunch money for school. His mom didn't like him doing that, but he insisted that was a way he could help her. He would do anything for his mom, who works hard to keep them in money to pay the bills and buy food.

Intriguing Escapade at Swim Camp

He loved being on the swim team. When he was at practice and had some time to watch other people, he always liked to watch Grace, Silver, Gold, and Lisa. There were good swimmers and was also pretty girls. He wished he could swim as good as those girls. Maybe he should practice more, but he wanted to work to help his mom with the bills.

Zeke thought Grace was the most beautiful girl in the world, and she's nice too. If I say 'hi' she always smiles and says it back. Not just everyone will do that. I heard she is a nice girl and a good girl. I think she goes to church. My mom would have taken me to church, but she always had to work all she could, and that included Sundays, but maybe that will be better soon.

Maybe I should look after these girls while we are here at the lake. I noticed they went inside that cave. He didn't know if that was a good idea or not, so he may have to follow them and keep them safe, if he sees them go in there again. He wouldn't want them to be harmed. He may play tricks on people, but deep down, he had a tender heart, and he for sure wouldn't play tricks to these girls who were so sweet.

Chapter Five

Grace has been on the swimming team for three years, but this is the first year she has had Coach Sheila for a coach. Grace likes her coach, but she has seen her be a bit too harsh to some of the girls. They couldn't help it if the coach expected something out of them that they couldn't do. Grace didn't know what to think about that. Coach had never been harsh to her, and she hoped it stayed that way. She didn't like it when Coach was not being nice to them, and Grace's mom would not like it at all if she was harsh to Grace.

Grace has an outstanding grandmama, who loves her very much. Her grandmama lives far away from Texas, but they get to see each other whenever they can. Her grandmama always comes to her meets when she is here, and if we are having one. She supports her swimming and, of course, and she thinks her granddaughter is the best swimmer in the water, and a champion.

Grace likes to swim and does it often. Her coach last year told her she was the best one on the team. She didn't know what to think about that either, but she enjoyed having her friends on the same team with her. They always had fun at school and when they were swimming most of all. They were all competitive and wasn't jealous of whoever won. If one of the friends beat the others, they always congratulated the winner, smiled, and patter her on the back.

She had a good family, and they all go to church together on Sundays. Grace got her learner's permit to drive, and much to her mom's despair, Grace often goes a touch too fast. Her dad told her she inherited that from her grandmama. She is sort of had a hot rod grandmama.

Grace was excited about the swim camp, because her friends would be going, and she knew they would have so much fun. They all liked to laugh and have fun together. Surely, they will have some free time other than just swimming. She couldn't wait for swim camp to begin.

She loved her older brother, but he liked to tease her, and she didn't like to be teased. One night at dinner she took a big swig of her water and noticed a big bug was in the bottom of her glass. Dear ole brother, put it in the glass right before dinner began. Grace picked up her glass and drew it back behind her head for the throw that was aimed at the head of her brother. Her dad took the glass out of her hand before she had an opportunity to toss it, so everyone proceeded to eat their dinner. That didn't happen too often, but they both liked teasing each other. She figured he was a pretty good brother, so she would keep him.

CHAPTER SIX

Silver and Gold were good friends to Grace and Lisa. They were on the same swim team as were the other two friends. Much fun was had when they were together, and they also couldn't wait to go to swim camp. They were good swimmers and when either of them won a competition over the other, the other one never got mad, which was great. The others were happy for the one who beat them.

Everybody often wonders when the twins meet new people, why they are named after metals from the ground. When the parents explain the reason, it makes sense. When they were born, a light was shining on their heads making one look like silver and the other looking like gold, so that is how the names came about. They knew they had odd names, but they were used to it.

Much to the dismay of the twin girls, they have triplet brothers, who like to aggravate their older sisters most of the time. They get into a lot of trouble and have all their little lives. The parents just think it's cute when they act up, unless it's something they do in public, then it's a bit different as the parents are truly embarrassed.

Intriguing Escapade at Swim Camp

"Silver, don't you think our parents should have drowned those boys at birth. They get in trouble all the time, and they aggravate the stew out of us," said a confused Gold, who didn't have a clue why boys acted this way. Gold thought boys were all crazy.

Gold heard the click of their bedroom door opening, "Get out of here, little brats. Mom, Mark, Luke, and John are in our room again," hollered Gold. That night the boys put a small snake in Gold's bed which didn't go over well with her. Silver got a chuckle out of it, but the boys did get into a little trouble with the parents over that little trick. Finally, the little brats were punished.

"Those boys are out of control," said Silver. "You saw what they did while the preacher was giving the message last Sunday." Silver couldn't believe why they didn't get in more trouble with that trick.

Luke reached in his pocket right in front of the preacher and pulled out a huge bullfrog and set it loose in the church. Aunt Bell saw it hopping down the middle of the aisle straight toward the preacher. Laughter broke out all over the church, even the preacher was laughing, but they guessed the preacher didn't know exactly know what to do either. Mom and dad didn't laugh at first, but after a while of the bullfrog hopping down the aisle, it became somewhat funny. Dear old dad figured he would have to dig deep in his pockets for a bunch of money to put in the offering plate to make up for this debacle.

When the huge bullfrog got beside Aunt Bell, it stopped and she jumped up on the pew holding her heart and hollering, "Lord, help me."

Mr. Bullfrog became tired of the floor and gave a big hop and landed on Cousin Pearl's bench, who was eighty, if she was a day. That's when Cousin Pearl ran out the back door quicker than a pig on the freeway. The whole way to the back door she was jumping around and stomping the floor on her way out. Everyone in the church was expecting a hallelujah out of Cousin Pearl at any time, but they were disappointed.

Mr. Bullfrog finally made it to the pulpit where good ole Preacher Bueler was trying to save his congregation by catching the bullfrog, but with no luck. Every time he got his hands on it, the frog gave a big ribbit and jumped out of his hands. The preacher appeared to be at a lose of what to do about all this.

Since it was his boys that started this disaster, the dad caught the frog and took it outside. Let's just say that dear ole dad wasn't very happy.

Chapter Seven

Lisa Acre was another one, who was best friends with Grace and the Gillygut twins. Her home life was somewhat different than the others. Her dad's work required him traveling to different places, and her mom always went with him wherever he went. They were gone, at least, three-quarters of each year leaving their daughter with the mail, who Lisa loved, but she had rather had her parents here with her, and they could go to her swim competitions, which they had never been to because they were never home, and when they were home, there was always something they had to do.

They had a considerable amount of money, so they had a live-in maid, who took care of Lisa when her parents were away. She didn't have any siblings, so she was often bored. That's why Lisa liked hanging out with her best friends. They all had siblings, and she didn't, and that's why she liked going to one of her friend's house. She liked to see them arguing with a brother when he teased them, or they would tease their brother making him go out in the garage to play his guitar where he wouldn't have them around.

Her parents didn't seem to care about anything she did, like swimming. They didn't go to the meets, even when they were home, which was unusual. She would love it just to see them in the bleachers even if they didn't know what was going on in the water. Maybe they could even yell for her, but she was afraid that was just a dream that may never come to be.

Grace and the twins always found special ways to make Lisa think she had sisters. Lisa was also excited to go to swim camp. She knew they would all have loads of fun. Grace and the twins made Lisa their honorary sister, and Lisa was happy about that. She was excited to be even an honorary sister.

Chapter Eight

The curious girls came out of the dark cave to return to the camp for dinner. When they got to camp, they noticed everyone was already there with cane poles in their hands. The late arrivals didn't have a clue what the cane poles were for or how that helped them with dinner. They thought they could watch the others and do like they do. The girls had never used a cane pole for their evening meal and were curious of what they would be doing.

"Okay ladies and gentlemen, we are having a wiener roast. I am going to give each of you a wiener to put on the end of your pole, and you will cook it over the fire. Be careful not to burn it. The buns, condiments, and drinks are on the table to your right. Don't throw away your pole because we will make smores for dessert," smiled Coach Sheila. They were excited about having to make smores. Now smores they knew how to do.

As they were eating, Zeke got Coach Sheila's attention and asked her if he could tell a ghost story while everyone ate their dinner. The girls thought Zeke was full of stories, and they probably wouldn't believe anything he said anyway. Everybody knew Zeke liked to play tricks on people.

"Go ahead, Zeke," said Coach who thought it was a stupid idea, but she would try to be nice and play along.

"Once long ago in a year where none of us were born, there was girl whose name was Mary Buford. She came here with her swim team and stayed here just like we are now. Like you, they were excited about being here. There was a girl, who seemed to have no friends and often sat alone at mealtimes, but she was the best swimmer on the team."

"Late one afternoon after the evening meal, Mary asked one of the girls if she wanted to go explore a cave she had seen after their practice was over. The girl told Mary she was afraid in dark places, so Mary set out to go by herself to see what she could find in a lonely, dark cave."

"It was time for 'lights out' as the coaches came in the girl's bunkroom. When they did a head count, they were puzzled because they were one short, so they did another count. They were becoming more and more worried. They had never lost a swimmer before and they didn't like this at all."

"Susie, who was the girl that Mary asked to go with her to the cave, told them about Mary and where she went. The coaches were beside themselves with anxiety. They immediately organized a search party to find Mary."

"The search party went over every inch of the cave with their flashlights and found nothing or nobody anywhere in the dark cave. To this very day, Mary has not been found. Some people, who go in the cave, swear they could hear splashing in the water, shadows on the walls of the cave of a female walking, and a girl crying, but still no one has ever found the girl named Mary."

Everyone finished their dessert and sauntered toward their bunkhouse for a good night's sleep because they had to be in the water by 9:30 the next morning. If they wanted breakfast, they needed to go to the firepit from last night around 8:30.

CHAPTER NINE

Before the giggly girls went to sleep, Grace had a question, "Hey girls, what did you think of the ghost story Zeke told us tonight?" The girls began giggling at that question. They didn't believe in ghosts, and they figured Zeke made up the whole story.

Lisa was the first to respond, "I don't exactly know what to think, because Zeke is always playing tricks on people. He does it all the time. He, most likely, thought he could scare someone. If anyone had actually ran away, then he would probably still be laughing. It would be a good trick.

Silver laughed as she looked at Grace and the others, "It very well could be a considerable amount of rubbish. What do you think, Gold?"

"It could be rubbish or maybe not. Why don't we ask him if he made this story up, or did he hear it somewhere?" explained Gold, who thought that was a logical answer. They could probably tell if he had made it up, because he has that smirk on his face when he plays a trick on someone. "He's hard to read sometimes."

Intriguing Escapade at Swim Camp

"It's not too late. We can look in the window of the boy's bunkhouse and try to get Zeke's attention, and we tell him to come outside, and we will tie him to a tree and torture him until he tells us the truth," laughed Lisa who thought that was a great idea. She had always wanted to do something like this. She hoped the others like that plan, because she really wanted to do this. She thought it would be so much fun to tie a boy to a tree.

"I like that plan," laughed Silver who couldn't seem to stop the laughter. She always enjoys a good adventure, and this one seemed to be a good one. "I think when he comes over to the window, we all together grab him and pull him out into the yard. That would make it even more adventurous."

Gold glanced at the other girls and smiled, "I saw some rope under one of the cots in our bunkhouse. Let's do this thing. He will never know what hit him. We need to pull him out the window as fast as we can."

Grace smiled and asked, "Are you sure this is a good thing to do?" Grace didn't have a mean bone in her body, but she smiled because she thought it would be fun.

"Grace, we know you have a good heart, but I promise we won't hurt him at all. We may just tickle him until he tells us about this story." Lisa didn't like being mean to people either. Grace is always the good influence, and the other girls respect that. They finally got good ole Grace to agree to do it. She thought it might be fun to play a trick on Zeke like he does everyone else.

They all finally agreed to try this. They ambled toward the door to their bunkhouse while trying not to giggle and wake everybody from their slumber. Poor ole Zeke will never know what hit him. Actually, the girls thought he just might enjoy this. In fact, they were sure of it.

They made it out the door and rambled toward the boys' bunkhouse. The closer they came to the boys' bunkhouse, they noticed one of the windows was open. The girls thought it was open because sometimes boys all together like this makes them stink. They finally saw where Zeke was, and Silver picked up a small stone and threw it at their target. Since she also played softball, she hit the person it was intended for.

Zeke felt the stone hit his neck and turned toward the window and saw the girls calling him over to the window. When he was in reach of the girls, four pair of arms grabbed him and pulled him through the window in record speed. They proceeded to walk him to a tree and began tying him to the tree. Of course, the girls giggled through the entire process. All four girls could barely contain their excitement at what they had just done. Zeke thought he would go along with whatever they had in mind. At least, they were paying attention to him. He knew it would be fun to see what they girls would do to him. They were smart, but not as strong as he was.

Silver looked Zeke in the eyes and smiled a wicked smile. She began walking in front of him like a New York lawyer with that silly grin hitting her hand with her stick. "Okay, Zeke Sheet, tell us how you know that this story of yours is true, or did you make it up and don't lie, or it will go much worse for you, and you don't want to mess with us."

"Are you going to beat me with that stick?" Zeke started laughing. "I like you girls. I won't lie to you."

Gold gazed at Zeke with a smirk, "Well, which is it? Do you tell us, or do we torture you?"

"One of the camp counselors told me that story. He thought it might scare me. It's the truth. I have something else to say. If you ladies go back to the cave tomorrow, I want to go with you. You may need a big strong man to protect you."

"Where do we get one of those, girls?" laughed Lisa as she stared at the boy tied to a tree.

They all laughed and told him he could go, but not tell anybody. They untied him, so he could get some sleep. "See you lovely ladies tomorrow." He laughed all the way back to his bunkhouse. He had finally got the attention of Grace, the twins, and Lisa.

CHAPTER TEN

The next morning was a hectic one at the Acre household. Lisa's parents came back from one of their European trips earlier than they expected. They thought they might spend some time with their daughter, who they don't see too often. Maybe they could take her to the playground at the park. She always loved to do that when she was little. It was like they thought she was still a little girl.

"Jack, should we take her to the playground? She might like that. How old is she now, Jack?" asked a confused Jill, who thought she should know how old that girl was, since she gave birth to her.

Jack sat deep in thought trying to remember how old his daughter was. "I think she may be up to thirteen by now, don't you think, Jill." Jack didn't know how old his daughter was either.

"I don't exactly know. Do you remember the year she was born?" said a smiling mommy dearest. "We should go upstairs to her bedroom and ask her."

"We can't do that. She will think we don't love her. I just remembered the year she was born. We were in Paris at a convention, and we had to go back home because you were almost ready to give birth. That would make her around fifteen by now." Jack was proud of himself for figuring that out.

"We need to go upstairs and wake her, so she will be surprised we are back," smiled Jill to Jack.

They slowly walked up the stairs to surprise their daughter. When they opened the door, they noticed she wasn't in the bed. "Maybe she is sleeping in our bed so she can feel closer to us." Jill thought that was a good idea, but when they went to their bedroom, she wasn't in there either, so they went to the kitchen, because she knew Lily, the maid, would be there preparing breakfast.

"Lily, Lily, where are you?" hollered Jack, who was confused about where his daughter could be.

They found Lily in the pantry doing an inventory or food products, "Lily darlin', where is our child?" Lily was overjoyed the parents were concerned about their daughter.

Lily smiled at the happy couple that she didn't see too often, "Ma'am, she is at the swim camp for a while. She will be back in a day or two."

"Why would she be in a swim camp. She can already swim," asked the confused Jack. Lily stopped what she was doing to explain why she was there practicing for a competition.

"How did she get there?" asked Lisa's mom. Jill was full of questions.

"I took her to Grace's house because her mom was going to take Lisa and the other three girls, who are her friends, to meet the bus to take them to the camp. It's just one county over, ma'am. She won't be there much longer, then you can pick her up when the bus returns to the school.

"Oh, that's so sweet. I didn't know Lisa had friends. We should invite them over sometime to dine with us," said Mom with a sweet smile. Jill means well, but she lacks in parenting skills from never being home most of the child's life.

"Yes, ma'am. I can make that happen when they return from camp," said Lily with a fake smile. She didn't like how they abandon their child so much. Lisa hardly knows them. She talks about them sometimes, but not too often. Lily knew Lisa had those same friends when she was in first grade. She felt sorry for Lisa, and as long as her parents are not home much, I will never leave her.

CHAPTER ELEVEN

Early the next morning, Coach Sheila was talking with the other coaches about the practice she wanted her students to do later this morning. The chaperons didn't agree with Sheila about the rigorous workout she was demanding they have. She was suggesting the workout be for five hours straight without a break. The other coaches were flabbergasted at her suggestion. They are kids and most kids don't have an attention span longer than a half hour.

The other coaches told her she could be reasonable, or they were going to leave and tell the parents why they are leaving. They were not going to do that to the kids. The kids needed them here to help, not to kill them. They would stay and take care of the swimmers and make sure they would be okay. No way would they leave the kids with Sheila.

Coach Sheila was about to go off the deep end and show what she is really like. Her temper was about to blow. She was fighting it because she knew if she lost her temper, she would be fired and sent on her merry way. She didn't know how she got in these fixes, but she tried hard, because she wants to keep her job.

She had already lost too many jobs, and this one may be her last if she loses her mind.

After much thinking about it, Sheila apologized to the other coaches, "I know all of you have been state champions and know what you are doing. I hope you all can forgive me. I guess I'm just tired. If you don't mind, I want you to do the practice for the rest of our stay here. I have to get myself under control. I will call my therapist today, and she can help me to calm down."

Hank looked at the others, and then looked at Sheila. "I have an idea. There are plenty of us, and we would take the whole class, girls and boys, and you can go back to your bed and rest. We can take care of practice for you the rest of the time we are here. We really enjoy it."

"Thank you so much. This is probably what I need today," Sheila knew this was the best thing for her. She didn't want everybody to see how she really is, because she truly didn't want to lose her job, and if she didn't get her therapist on the phone, she would keep calling. She had to get herself under control.

Sheila walked back to the bunkhouse where the adults were staying and found her phone. She needed to call her therapist and talk this out. She put in the number, but it rang and rang, so she left a message. "Hello, this is Sheila, and I really need your help today. I almost lost it with some other coaches. Please call me back." She was sure she would receive a call soon. Her therapist has never let her down.

The other coaches didn't know what to think about Coach Sheila. They had never come across this kind of situation before, but they would take care of the kids, because they didn't think Sheila would care what the kids were doing.

CHAPTER TWELVE

The kids ate a small breakfast that consisted of Twinkies and a bottle of water. They thought Coach Sheila must not know how to cook. After that nutritious breakfast, they made their way to the lake. The saw the coaches already there, but no Coach Sheila. That was okay because they like the other coaches too. They were nice to all the kids and helped them so much while they were in practice. They told us things to do that Coach Sheila never told them.

Grace, Silver, Gold, Lisa, and Zeke couldn't wait for practice to end, so they could change their clothes and go to the cave. They were hoping no one knew they were going to the cave, because they didn't want the whole group to be in there. It was much too small for that.

Practice was over and the group of cave people agreed to meet in the back of the boys' bunkhouse in twenty minutes. They all ran to get out of wet swimsuits and into dry clothes. They couldn't wait to see what they may find today in the dark scary cave.

"Hey Grace, what are you girls going to do this afternoon?" asked a girl named Susie who was on their swim team. Susie was a nice girl, and a good swimmer, and all the girls like her.

Grace looked at her friends and smiled. She had a plan. "We are going ziplining later on today. Maybe we will see you there, Susie."

"Good answer, Grace," said Silver with a smile. "Susie is a good girl."

In exactly twenty minutes, they all met out back of the bunkhouse. Zeke's smile was huge, because he was so happy the girls were letting him go to the cave with them. He liked these girls because they were so much fun to be around, and he hoped they would let him be in their group. They arrived at their destination and slowly ambled to the mouth of the cave. Everyone got their phones and turned on the flashlight.

Zeke volunteered to go in first, and the girls were okay with that. The girls followed him without making a sound. They noticed the part that looked somewhat like a bench from yesterday. They could hear running water and went toward the sound. It looked like a stream of some kind, and they wondered where it went. There was no ocean for it to go in, so maybe it runs into the lake. They would have to look around the lake and find it to see if it's coming out there.

Intriguing Escapade at Swim Camp

All five of the kids stood completely still and listened. The sound of someone whistling was beginning to give them chills. They knew that from the ghost story Zeke told everyone last night. Surely, it is not true, but they all heard the whistling. They didn't know what to think until a small light was shining and they could see the shadow of a girl. Wow! Now, it was really getting spooky in the cave.

"You think it is Mary?" asked Gold, who really wanted to run out of here, but she would stay with the others. A ghost probably couldn't hurt people anyway. It still would be scary, but they could always run out the mouth of the cave. She would do what the others did, because she knew Silver wouldn't let her be harmed. She was a good twin sister. It was not making Gold comfortable being in there.

Silver glanced at the eyes of the others and noticed they were somewhat larger as they gazed at the wall, "Listen people, that could be someone who put a light in here with a silhouette of a girl, and the loud whistling could be on a recorder, and it all has been set with a timer. You can buy those things at Walmart. Someone did this so people would really think the story was true, and most likely to keep people out of the cave for whatever reason. No matter what it was, it was making them all jittery.

"I think Silver is right about all this. They probably don't want people in here, so they set this up to scare people away," said Zeke, who was hoping he was right. Zeke wasn't the strong boy they thought he was. He thought this all was somewhat weird, but mostly, he thought someone did this on purpose to scare people away, but he couldn't imagine why.

"You're right, Zeke and Silver." They all agreed to leave, but that's when they heard what sounded like men talking and laughing. "We need to follow that. There are actually some people back there somewhere. We need to check it out. Come on", said Zeke, who liked a good adventure. The girls couldn't imagine why someone would be back in a cave. They had to be up to no good. At least, that is what Grace's dad would tell her, so now they were all had doubts, except Zeke.

Grace smiled, "I have an idea. If you want to make it more interesting, we need to go do the ziplining, and then come back later before dinner to check out the voices."

"I'm in," said the rest of the group.

Chapter Thirteen

The happy group walked back to the camp for lunch. They hoped it wasn't another Twinkie for lunch. The closer they got to the camp, they smelled the aroma of grilled hamburgers, which was okay with all the campers. The group who went to the cave were starving. They thought cave searching must make a person hungry because they thought they could eat a whole cow by now.

Silver smiled at her group, "It shouldn't take too long to eat and zipline. That way we can be at the cave before it gets dark. What do you yahoos think about that plan?" She really wanted to do the zipline before dark.

They all agreed with Silver's plan which made her smile. They knew they had to go ziplining because the others might get suspicious of why they didn't do it. They others didn't need to know what they were doing. It wasn't any of their business. It was going to be their secret, and no one else needed to know what they had been doing. They wanted to keep all this fun to themselves.

They all had a couple of burgers each and decided that was enough for them. They began trekking toward the zipline. They noticed almost everybody was there and having a grand old time. It was a long zipline that went over the lake and then over the top of some trees. All the cave group had been ziplining before, except for Zeke. They understood why because his mom had to work a lot, and she didn't have time to take him. They watched as Zeke had his turn to zipline. They wanted to make it fun for him.

Grace had another idea, "While we are up above the lake, we need to look to see if we notice water coming into the lake from the cave. Then we will know where that water goes. If someone tries to get us, we can swim right into the lake that is close to our bunkhouse."

"Great idea, Grace. I agree with her, girls. What about you ladies?" said a smiling Zeke, who couldn't wait to do a lot of ziplining. He thought ziplining would be better than being in a dark cave.

"It's okay with the rest of us," said Silver, who was speaking for them all. She knew they would all agree anyway.

As Zeke began his zipping, the girls began hollering for him. "You go, Zeke." Zeke was laughing out loud as he zipped along, loving every minute of it. It made the girls happy to see him that happy. They would need to do more things with Zeke. The way his mom and him work, he doesn't have much time for fun.

They all finished their ziplining and walked back toward the bunkhouses so everyone wouldn't see them going toward the cave.

Intriguing Escapade at Swim Camp

As they entered the cave, they still heard loud talking and laughing, which sounded like a bunch of men. They noticed a small trail, so they followed it. The more they walked, the louder the laughing was. Using their flashlights on their phones, they found a small door over to the left of the cave.

"Look at that door. It looks like a Hobbit door. It's so cute," laughed Grace as she gazed at the door while wondering why a Hobbit door would even be in a cave. She was sure there were no Hobbits in there, but it was a fun thought. She just hoped it wasn't bad men in the cave. It wasn't a very big place, and she wasn't too sure they could get out of there in a hurry, if needed.

"Wow!" said Lisa, who couldn't wait to see what was on the other side of that cute door. "We know it's men laughing, so we need to be careful. They have to be up to no good, or they wouldn't be hiding inside a cave. I just hope it's not a bunch of serial killers." Lisa was on a roll today, because she was elated to be with her friends doing crazy stuff. If her friends thought it was okay to be here, then she was okay with it too.

"Now, that didn't make us feel better. Although, I wouldn't think there is such a thing as a Serial Killer convention," smiled Grace as she looked at her friends. They all began laughing but tried not to be too loud.

"I'll open it just a small crack, so we can see what is going on, but we need to be ready to run in case they see us. It could be something illegal they are doing in there, and they sure wouldn't want to be found out if that is the case," said Zeke. They girls thought Zeke was making a great deal of sense, so they would go with that plan. Zeke seemed to be a smart boy. The girls thought that was due to staying by himself while his mom was at work.

He slowly pushed on the door and made a small crack so they all could see inside. Men were in there gambling and there were bookies taking bets on ballgames. Man, oh man, this has got to be illegal gambling. No wonder they are doing it somewhere that law enforcement wouldn't even think about something like this going on inside a cave.

Gold was curious about all that, "Is that stuff illegal?" She had a horrified look on her face as she asked that.

"Yep," said Silver. "We can't let them see us. If this is illegal, they will probably kill us. We need to get out of here. They might think we would go tell someone what they were doing and then it wouldn't be good for them at all.

"Hey, there are kids watching us. Let's get'um," said a man named Buck. Several of the men got up from their chair and came toward the door. The kids were in trouble now. They knew they had to run and run fast.

Intriguing Escapade at Swim Camp

The five kids who thought they were going to die, ran faster than they ever had before. They ran out of the cave and went the wrong way from the camp. They almost ran over an old woman, who smiled at them and said, "Come with me if you need to hide. My cabin is not far away. RUN!" The kids were amazed because the old woman was running faster than they were.

Chapter Fourteen

The gambling men ran out the Hobbit door to catch the kids. Maybe they could scare them into not telling anyone what they saw. Getting caught for illegal gambling was not an option for them. They have been doing this for a year now, and they haven't been caught. Not many people come inside this cave, but if we have to be caught, they didn't want it to be because of a group of teenagers. We can't let those kids get away. As they were looking all around them, they didn't see the teenagers anywhere. There was no place to hide, so the men couldn't understand where they could be. Maybe they can just run faster than most kids because of all the swimming.

"What do you think, Buck. Do you have any idea where they could be?" asked his friend who helped Buck start this business. It has made them a considerable amount of money, and they didn't want to stop now.

Buck sat rubbing his chin as he thought of where the teenagers could be, "I think I may know where they are. There is a swim camp not far from here, and groups of kids come here to help improve their swimming skills for competitions. That is the only place I know of unless they jumped on the zipline cables. I saw them practicing yesterday, and there were a lot of kids there, but there were also several coaches helping them too, who looked like they were strong. If they were also swimmers, they would be strong as well."

"There is no way the coaches will let us in the bunkhouses, so that's not an option. We may need to wait until tomorrow to search for them. They are probably too scared tonight to say anything to anyone," said Buck as he walked back to the gambling room with Joseph. Buck couldn't believe this was happening. They had such a good thing going for a year, and along comes a bunch of kids, and it could all be over, and they may go to jail. This was turning out not to be a good day, and all because of a bunch of teenagers. They would find them eventually. They couldn't hide forever.

"Good idea. I'm getting hungry enough to eat a possum. The first thing tomorrow we should go to the swim camp. They probably do swimming exercises in the mornings," said Joseph. It may be better to sneak into their bunkhouse at night when people will be asleep. I think we got a good enough look at them to recognize them even if their eyes are closed." Joseph liked that plan.

Buck looked at his friend and smiled, "I really don't think we have anything to worry about, because those kids most likely won't come back inside that cave, and who in their right mind would believe them even if they did tell someone. So, I think we will be okay. We should be good without doing anything."

"If you think it will be okay, then I trust you," smiled Joseph, who sure hoped Buck was right.

Chapter Fifteen

Peculiar thoughts were rolling around inside the minds of the five swimming competitors as they ran away with this quirky woman, who was running faster than the teenagers, who thought this lady must be in her eighties or nineties. They had no idea where she was taking them until they noticed a run-down cabin was up ahead. The cabin would probably be demolished if a strong wind blew in. At this point in time, they didn't care if the cabin bore a resemblance to an outhouse, as long as it provided them with a safe place away from men who had been chasing them out of the cave. They didn't know what was on the minds of the men, but it couldn't go well for the teenagers.

The teenagers went inside the lady's cabin and stared in wonder how the cabin was even standing upright. The boards on the wall had worm holes, and at all appearances were rotten. The swimmers noticed something hanging from the rafters and the same thing was hanging on the front porch. The teens were curious but were polite and didn't want to hurt her feelings. After all, she may have saved their life from the gambling men when she took them away from the cave.

The odd little lady took a gander at the kids and said, "By the way, my name is Izzy. You may call me Izzy." The girls wanted to giggle, but they didn't want to hurt their hostess. They thought she was nice, even if she was somewhat strange.

This was confusing Grace, so she politely asked, "Ma'am, what is that hanging from the rafters and on the front porch? I don't know if I have seen anything like that before. I'm sure it has a good purpose, or you wouldn't have it there."

The little old lady, who seemed sort of odd, smiled, "Ma'am? Did you hear that? She called me ma'am. Nobody calls me ma'am. I may be called a bunch of other names, but not ma'am." She looked at Grace and told her she was so sweet as she began to pinch Grace's cheeks. Grace didn't know what to do, so she just sat and smiled while the old lady kept pinching her cheeks that was becoming a bright pink with each pinch. She knew the others would be laughing because they would think it was funny, and it actually was. Even Grace, who was getting 'cheek pinched' thought it was funny, although, it was hard to laugh with your cheeks being pinched.

Zeke laughed, "Yep, she sure is sweet." Then he proceeded to pinch Grace's cheeks, who thought her cheeks were bruised about now. She was going to go home with blue cheeks, and she didn't know what her parents would think of that. They would probably think it was funny too.

Intriguing Escapade at Swim Camp

The strange lady gazed at her guest, "I'll answer your question, Grace. That stuff hanging is garlic to keep vampires away. Did you see any vampires when you were in the cave?" At first, Grace didn't have any idea what to say to that statement. She really didn't believe in vampires, and if there were vampires, she didn't know about garlic shooing them away, but she wouldn't say anything because she might start pinching her cheeks again, and Grace didn't think she could take much more of that.

The teenagers were throwing glances at each other with broad smiles. The thoughtful teenagers were thinking the old lady was a little off her rocker. Silver answered her question with a smile that turned into a small giggle. They were really enjoying this crazy lady. "Ma'am, we didn't see any vampires today. They may have been asleep. Don't they sleep during the day?"

"You're right, little lady. They do sleep during the day because they can't stand the sunlight, but you don't need to be scared, because I will take care of you kids," said the old lady with a huge laugh. She wasn't going to let any vampires hurt her knew friends. The teens didn't have many words to say about all that was being said in this strange conversation.

The kids didn't believe in vampires, ghosts, or goblins, but they would play along with this clueless old lady, because she didn't seem to have it all going on upstairs, but she was interesting and fun.

"Oh, oh, where are my manners? You kids sit down here at the table. You are probably thirsty from all that running. I can't believe I forgot to offer you something to drink. I have just the thing for you. It will nourish you and give you the energy you need to go back to your swimming camp," smiled the old woman who was ninety, if she was a day.

The teenagers didn't really want to, but they didn't want to hurt her feelings. They noticed she was dragging some extra chairs around the long table, which was confusing to her guests. They wondered how many people were in this cabin, and it made them want to run until the old lady brought in more guests. The old lady wanted to share her family with the kids. She thought they would like them.

Empty chairs were being filled as the silent teens sat with opened mouths in amazement at the sight before them. This sure never had this happened to them before, and they couldn't wait to see how this all played out. It is truly a something they would not forget at the home of Miss Izzy. Miss Izzy came out with her family with a smile as big and bright as the sun.

Chapter Sixteen

Buck and Joseph ran back to the cave and through the Hobbit door. Frustration was running high in the gambling room as the men were becoming fearful they would be found, and possibly incarcerated.

Buck looked at the others in the room, "We need a plan of some sort. These teenagers need to be scared away with a threat of death if they tell anyone. Teenagers will believe it and won't know the men would never hurt them. It was really mean of the men, but they didn't know anything else to do.

Joseph agreed with Buck, because it was Buck and him who started this gambling room, and they were not going to let some kids, who were still 'wet behind the ears' ruin it for them. They would do what they needed to do, so they could continue their gambling room. They made good money and didn't want that ruined.

"What do you think we should do, Joseph? Any ideas?" asked Buck with a worried look on his craggy face. He knew his wife would probably leave him if she found out about him doing this in the first place. He loved his wife and didn't want her to leave and live with her insane sister, so he would make sure she never found out about all this. If they get caught, he would be in jail, and his wife would leave him, for sure. She has threatened to do it before, but now, she wouldn't hesitate.

Joseph sat appearing to be deep in thought, "These teenagers may be a part of the swim camp that is not too far from here. I noticed some teams were practicing in the lake yesterday. Perhaps we should go there tonight and scare them. I noticed there were four girls and one boy. We could take the boy and bring him back here and let the girls know we are taking him and if they talk, they will hurt him bad." Joseph thought that might work, and if it didn't, they would have to think of something else even worse to do to the boy and maybe the girls too.

"I like that idea. It should work, Joseph. We can wait until it's their bedtime and sneak in the bunkhouses," explained a hopeful Buck. At least, that was Buck was wishing for. He was hoping they did not lock the doors at night, but just in case, they might need to take some sort of tool to get the door unlocked. One way or another, they were going to get that boy and bring him back to the gambling room and tie him to something so he can't run away.

Five of the other men in the room stood up and walked up to Buck and told him they did not want to get into any trouble with the law. They were in another illegal gambling room before and it was raided. The police took all of them in the room to the police station.

Intriguing Escapade at Swim Camp

The police talked to us and explained that they shouldn't be there gambling because it was against the law, but the ones who started the gambling hall had to stay. They did not know what happened to them, but they didn't want any part of this again. Buck and Joseph didn't want to even try to get a license, and that is the reason they are in a cave.

Chapter Seventeen

Jack and Jill Acre decided they would go to the camp to retrieve their daughter and bring her back home with them. She should have been here to greet us when we returned. Jill didn't know if this was usual behavior for a teenager or not. Maybe they should see her more often, and they would know these things. Perhaps they could buy a book of some kind on how teenagers are wired, or they could ask Grace's parents. They think her parents stay at home all the time, and actually take their children with them when they go on vacations. Maybe they could take their daughter on a vacation some time.

"Jack, are we not raising our daughter correctly? Maybe we should stay home more often and be with her," Jill seemed to be confused about all this parenting business. It was turning out to be more involved than they thought when she was a baby. Jill thought it was a lot of trouble with a small baby, but this teenager thing is a different ballgame.

"We could stay more often. I will tell my office to give me less trips to make. I believe I would like that. It would be sort of an early retirement kind of thing," Jack seemed to be happy with that decision. He thought it was time, because it bothered him more than Jill will ever know how much it bothered him not to know his own daughter. He thought taking a job that required a lot of traveling wasn't a good idea for people with children.

"You're right, Jack. I just remembered that Lisa is now fifteen years old. Where has the time gone. Do you think she would even want us here, since we have not been good parents in the past? We might even go to one of those swimmy things she does. Yes, I think she might like that. Time will tell. We may like this thing called parenting. She wanted them to be good parents, and ones she would like along with love.

Lily sat in the kitchen and listened to her employers talk about staying home more with Lisa. That made Lily smile, because she knew Lisa would love to have her parents around more often. She worried about Lisa because she was often unhappy about not having parents like her other friends. A brother or sister would have been nice too, but she knew they had chosen not to have more children.

"Lily, we are going to see Lisa at that camp. We probably will be bringing her back with us," said Jill, who really wanted to be a good mom, but she didn't know how, but she was willing to learn.

"Ma'am, could I make a suggestion? Lisa may not want to come back with you tonight, because since she is there with her friends, she will be having fun with them and may want to stay. She will only be there another day or two," explained Lily who thought it was sad that she knew more about Lisa more than her parents did.

"Good idea, Lily. I wouldn't know what we would do without you," said Jack with a smile.

The parents drove to the swim camp where Lisa was with her friends. They got out of the car and saw Lisa's swim coach. She asked where Lisa might be right now. Coach Sheila told the parents that it may be a while before Lisa and her friends would be back.

"The kids are on a break now and free to explore and go ziplining. They should be back around an hour or two," explained Coach Sheila.

"Oh fun, we will go into town and do a few things and come back later. Thank you so much for your kindness," said Jill with a smile. She might just start liking this parenting thing.

CHAPTER EIGHTEEN

The group of teenagers from the swim camp sat quietly watching Izzy bring her family out of the back room. First, she brought a cute little monkey, who was wearing blue overalls, and sat it in the chair. Next, came a baby tiger wearing a diaper, with no teeth that Izzy put in a chair and tied it to the back because she said the tiger was a baby and had lots of energy. The next one was a pig in a tutu, who had its own chair, and last came a huge snake with no clothes. The teenagers began to get out of their chairs until Izzy told them that none of her babies would harm them. The teens sitting at the table with a crazy woman and a variety of animals, didn't know what to say, so they sat quietly wondering what was going to be next in this house. The animals, and the garlic for keeping vampires away, was a little extreme to the confused teenagers.

The teenagers sat back down although they were still skeptical about sitting with this menagerie of animals Izzy brought out for their treat. Izzy had a huge smile on her face because she thought she was giving the kids a treat by showing them her babies. The teens wouldn't exactly called them babies, but they would never tell their hostess that. They thought she had to be out of her mind, but maybe she is just lonely.

"Ladies, and gentleman, I would like to introduce you to my babies. The monkey is Mikey, the tiger is named Tigger, the pig's name is Oink, and the snake is called Sneaky. The swimmers couldn't say much because Izzy was so proud to introduce them to her guests. The teens were good little guests and didn't say what they would like to say, but they wouldn't not hurt Izzy's feelings, because she had been nice to them, and she was so happy to be able to show them her babies.

Izzy brought each of the teenagers a glass of something liquid, while Mikey got a banana, Tigger got a huge piece of meat, which confused the kids because Tigger didn't have any teeth, but who were they to judge. Oink got some corn, and Sneaky got a dead rat.

The teenagers didn't have a clue about what to do next, so they started to drink their glass of whatever it was. Silver took a drink first and almost chocked to death. "Wow! Miss Izzy. That's pretty powerful. What is it exactly?" Silver thought it was the most disgusting thing she had ever had in her mouth, and it didn't do anything for her thirst. She wanted to ask if she had a bottle of water, but again, she didn't want to hurt Izzy's feelings. Her mama had taught her better than that.

Intriguing Escapade at Swim Camp

"Darlin' that is a hefty glass of vinegar. Drink up, it's good for the soul and the gout." They all drank a small sip and thought that would be enough, but Izzy told them to drink up because they would need energy to go back to the camp. They did as they were told, and it made Izzy smile. They thought she may not have much company and didn't know what she should give them, but she probably didn't have much money to buy stuff, so they wouldn't complain.

"Oh no, I forgot Witchy. Where is my little Witchy? I bet she's in the tree again. Excuse me, but I will have to shimmy up the tree and get Witchy. She loves vinegar." She walked out the door, as did the teenagers, because they had never seen a ninety-year-old woman shimmy up a tree before. She went up and came back down with a kitten, who they thought must be Witchy. This day couldn't get any stranger, but it was amazing to see an old woman shimmy up a tall oak tree.

Izzy sat Witchy down in a chair, who was a dark black cat with huge green eyes. Witchy must have belonged to a witchy woman before coming to live with Izzy. Witchy got a dead rat for her meal too. The teenagers were beginning to like Izzy. She was different, for sure, but she was fun to be around. She liked doing fun things.

"Miss Izzy, we have enjoyed being here with you, but we need to return to our swim camp for our evening meal. We want to thank you so much for your help in getting us away from the men who were chasing us, and for the tasty vinegar. You may have just saved our lives and we appreciate that.

"I want you sweet kids to come back and see me before you go home to your parents. You tell your parents that I said they did a good job in raising you children." That's when Miss Izzy gave out a loud witches' yell and said in a witchy voice, "I never ate me a sweet child." All of the five teenagers ran out the door of Izzy's house, jumped off the porch, and ran as fast as they could toward the swim camp to eat their dinner. They sure didn't want to be Izzy's dinner.

Izzy watched them running back and began laughing. She sure liked to scare kids, but she wouldn't dare eat one, but they didn't have to know that. They thought it was so much fun watching the kids run when she said she would like to eat a sweet kid. Izzy smiled the rest of the day at the sweet teenagers who came to visit.

Chapter Nineteen

As the teenagers were running back to the camp for their evening meal, they got stopped by a man wearing a coonskin cap, who must have been seven-feet tall. "Hey kids, are you scared of something. I won't hurt you. Are you the kids I saw some men chasing earlier today?" They thought this man might help them if that was to happen again, which they hoped it didn't happen again.

"Yes Sir, it was us. We didn't know what they were going to do to us, so we ran, and an old lady took us to her cabin so we would be safe. She was kind of odd, but we stayed for a little bit," said Zeke, who liked this man's cap. Besides having a cool-looking cap, he was around seven feet tall. He had a nice personality and most of his teeth.

For some reason, the teenagers trusted this man. "You were at Izzy's cabin, weren't you?" They all shook their heads but were speechless.

"Yes Sir," smiled Grace, who thought everybody around these parts know Miss Izzy. She is an oddity and not easily forgotten.

"That old bat is crazier than a Bessie bug. She won't hurt you, but she is odd, for sure. I guess living there by herself with only a few animals to keep her company keeps her a touch crazy," said the nice man in the coonskin cap.

"My name is Rusty, and I live just over that small hill with my wife and ten kids. If those mean men chase you again, you go to my house and we will protect. I know all about those men who are doing the illegal gambling. You must have been in the cave and found out what they were doing, or they wouldn't be chasing you. Is that right?"

Gold hasn't spoken since she saw Izzy bring out the huge snake. It must have knocked out all the air out of her lungs, "Yes Sir."

"Okay kids, I was serious when I said to run to my house if they chase you again, and if you need my help, I'll be glad to help anyway I can. It's not right for grown men to chase teenagers. I wouldn't want them chasing my kids like that, so remember what I said about helping if I need to. I'm not too fond of the gambling men, because one of them knocked down two of my kids. It was completely uncalled for, because they didn't do anything to them, and they wouldn't have known what they were doing even if they had seen them.

Intriguing Escapade at Swim Camp

"If you do come to my house, don't be afraid of my wife, Ruby. She was in a tree trying to chase out a possum for supper and fell out of the tree right on her head, and she hasn't been too sane since. She sings church hymns most of the day, but she has a good voice, and she sings good ole gospel songs. She won't harm you," explained Rusty. "She loves our babies and is a good woman."

"Thank you, Mr. Rusty," said Grace, and then the teenagers started back to the swim camp for supper. "We sure will take you up on your offer to help us, and your house shouldn't be too hard to find. Although, we hope it doesn't happen again."

They all said goodbye to Rusty and hurried back toward their camp. They were teenagers and they were starving. They sure were hoping it was going to be a good dinner tonight. They were getting a little tired of hot dogs and hamburgers.

Chapter Twenty

Rusty slowly walked back to his house because his work was over for the day. He needed to check on Ruby and the kids. His house wasn't much to look at, but it had kept the rain off them for twenty years. They had everything they could ever want. He made sure of that. They didn't need a mansion here on Earth because they could wait and get their mansion in Heaven. They were doing fine and didn't need fancy stuff all around them. His wife and kids were enough for him.

He sometimes worried about Ruby because ever since her accident, she hasn't been the same. She's still the sweetest voice and prettiest girl that's ever been in his life, and he will take care of her no matter what happens. At least, she still knows the kids and me, and she smiles all day long.

He finally made it to the house, and when he walked in the door, he started hollering for his kids, "Bobbie, Robbie, Tonya, Sonya, Will, Bill, Maggie, Susie, Tommy, Faith, daddy's home." The kids always loved it when daddy was home from work, because sometimes he stops and get them candy.

Intriguing Escapade at Swim Camp

"Yeah," said all the kids as they ran to meet their dad coming home from work. He does this every day, because he may have a lot of kids, but he loved each of them just the same. They gave him joy.

"Ruby," he walked in the kitchen and found his wife cooking supper. "Mother, we may have some company. I saw some of those gambling men we have been seeing and they were chasing some teenagers away from the cave and they have been with crazy Izzy."

"I hope they weren't hurt, Rusty. Can we help in any way?" said Ruby with a smile. All her life, she has had a tender heart and a good disposition, and this accident didn't mess with any of that.

"Yes, I saw the kids, and I told them if the men started chasing them again, for them to come to our house and hide. Is that okay with you, Ruby?"

"Yes. I would love to have them here if they need to be," said Ruby with a sweet smile on her pretty face.

Rusty heard Ruby singing *Amazing Grace* as he walked out the door to the barn to feed the horses. He smiled because she had a sweet voice, and it was better for her to sing instead of crying all day like some people do when they land on their head. Jo Jo told him his mother did the same thing when she fell out of the tree, and all she does is run around the outside of the house most of the day, but he wished she did sing instead of running. At least, she will be in shape.

Rusty thought he had been blessed that Ruby just sang gospel songs instead of running around the house. She still had most of the brain capacity but had lost just a small portion of it. She would be okay.

He was hoping the teenagers will take him up on his offer if they need help. He sure didn't want them to be hurt because he didn't know what the men would do to them since they found out what they were doing. The men will be afraid the kids will tell on them and they may go to jail. In his opinion, they all needed to go to jail. He takes a pitiful man to want to chase teenagers and threaten them with harm.

Chapter Twenty-One

The tired teenagers strolled back to the swim camp for their evening meal, hoping they didn't have vinegar to drink instead of soda. The day had been a long one with everything they had done so far. The swim practice early this morning was great. Not only did they enjoy the practice, but they learn some new things from the championship coaches. They liked the coaches who came to help. It wasn't that Coach Sheila was a bad coach, but these extra coaches make it so much fun, and they don't holler at the kids. Coach Sheila always hollered at the kids in a mean voice like it was going to make a difference. Some of the parents had been complaining about her to the people at the natatorium. They didn't like a lot of things Coach Sheila was doing.

"What did you think of our encounter with the crazy lady this morning?" asked Gold with a sneaky smile. She didn't know about the others, but she thought she was funny. She had never seen anyone like this strange lady before. "I know she was old. That may be what older women do."

Silver glanced at her sister and said, "I liked her because she was different and had a couple dozes of crazy in her, plus she was funny. Where do you think you would find a toothless baby tiger?" It amazed the teenagers that this crazy lady had so many animals that most people wouldn't even consider putting in their house, but Miss Izzy called them her babies.

Zeke started laughing, "I thought she was a hoot. I've never seen anyone like her, and probably won't ever see one like her again. The only thing I didn't like was having to drink some vinegar. I mean, who in their right mind drinks vinegar? I hope I never have that experience again in my lifetime." Zeke looked at the others who were laughing at him. It didn't bother him any because he liked it when people laughed.

Grace laughed right along with the others, "She was crazy and funny, and I would like to visit her again if we have time." Grace also thought the lady was funny, but somewhat odd. She had never seen anyone like her before.

Everyone agreed she was fun to be around, even if she was a touch insane. Lisa had a question, "Did you see that old woman shimmy up the tree to get the witch's cat? That lady has to be ninety. I wonder how she climbs up in a tree so fast, or at her age, how she goes up the tree at all."

"I thought it was nice of that kind man to offer his help if we need it. At least, now we have somewhere safe if we need it, or we could go back and see Old Mother Hubbard," laughed Zeke, who was happy the girls were letting him hang with them. Zeke was so happy he would almost agree with anything.

As they walked inside the swim camp, Lisa saw something she never thought she would see here at a camp. It was her parents sitting in the outside chairs. She didn't think her mother would ever be in a wooded area. She was not an outdoor person, but here she was sitting in a lawn chair. Whatever the reason they were here, she was happy to see them. They had been gone for a long time without even a phone call to her, but she would forgive them because they are, after all, her parents, but at least, one phone call would have been good.

Lisa ran up to her parents and hugged them, "I thought you weren't going to be home until next month. What happened?" Lisa waited for their answer.

Her dad told her to sit down because there was something they wanted to talk to her about, "Honey, we are going to cut back on our trips, so we can spend more time with you. We will be home more and would love to go to your swimming competitions." Her parents didn't have a clue how elated she was when her dad made that statement. She couldn't believe it. They had been gone for most of her life, and now they are going to be here more. Perhaps she will get to know them better.

"That's great. I would love that, and I'm so happy you will be home more." Lisa was so happy, she had tears in her eyes. She didn't think this day would ever come, but it has, and she couldn't be happier about it. There is so much she wanted to talk to them about, and things she wanted to do with them.

"I know you have some friends. Was that the ones you just came in the camp with?" asked her smiling mom. "We would love to meet them."

"Yes, it was. We have been friends since the first grade," laughed Lisa as she glanced over at her friends who knew her parents wasn't home much, and they noticed how happy Lisa was now that they were here. The tired friends overheard Lisa's dad tell her they would be home more now. They were so happy for their friend, because they knew Lisa needed that happiness.

"I would like to have them over for dinner one night, so we can become acquainted. Are they all on your swim team?" asked Mom.

"Thank you, mom," said Lisa as she hugged her parents again. "Are you both staying for our evening meal?"

"No, we have to go home and unpack, but we will be there when you return home from camp. We will see you then, bye darling. Have fun," said her dad as he hugged his daughter so hard, the friends thought Lisa's eyes might pop out of their sockets at any moment.

Chapter Twenty-Two

After eating their dinner of pizza and cheese bread, they walked over to the firepit to roast some marshmallows. When one of the boys sat in one of the chairs, it gave off a loud sound of a fart which was made from a whoopie cushion. Grace and her friends automatically looked at Zeke, because they knew how he liked to trick people. Zeke glanced back at the girls with a sneaky smile. Yep, it was Zeke. The girls thought it was somewhat funny that he liked to prank everybody.

The girls looked at Zeke and laughed. They thought it was juvenile, but apparently that is what boys do, so they forget about it, as they do their eyeroll and walk away. The girls walked back toward their bunkhouse for some much-needed rest. Around the side of the building, they heard the coaches talking. They tiptoed a little closer so they could listen to what they were saying. They thought they may be talking about who they think are good swimmers, but when they heard the conversation, they were having, it was not about that at all. It seemed to be pointed at Coach Sheila and that really perked up the teens' ears.

Intriguing Escapade at Swim Camp

Now the girls were even more interested to listen to what they may say about their coach. Maggie and Bell had been on the computer and decided to look up Coach Sheila's credentials, and they did not like what they found. It appeared the coach was fired from her other positions for being abusive to some of her students. It says here she broke a girl's hand when she pushed her into a block wall.

Grace, the twins, Lisa, and Zeke listened with fear on their faces. They could not believe this had happened. First, they come upon an illegal gambling room, drink vinegar with a strange lady with strange animals in her house, and now Coach Sheila is not what she seems to be. This was beginning to make the teenagers upset because they didn't know what to do now.

Chapter Twenty-Three

Zeke told the girls he was going to get his computer and look up Miss Sheila on the website. He brought it to the girls' bunkhouse, and they all stared in wonder at the screen where it said these things were true. To the swimmers, who just found out some bad news, this had been a strange day so far.

Grace looked at her friends and said, "I don't have any idea what we should do with this information we learned tonight. I sure do not think my parents would like it, and probably your parents wouldn't like it either. We need to think about all this before we do anything. If we tell, and coach finds out we know about her, she may hurt us too. Why don't we sleep on it? We need rest, so we can go to practice in the morning and try to keep a neutral face when we see Coach Sheila." They thought that might be the best thing to do right now. It would be hard, but they would do their best not to let her know they found out her secret.

"It has been a long day, and I'm a little tired, but then again, after hearing all this about Coach Sheila, I don't know if I can sleep or not," said Silver, as she put her arm around her sister's shoulders, who was beginning to have tears in her tired eyes. Gold was a little more tender than Silver.

Lisa looked at her compadres and said, "This is a lot to take in and hard to believe, but the other coaches said it, and then Zeke looked her up, and it said the same thing the coaches had said. Should we talk to the coaches and see if they will have any idea of what we should do?"

"We could go to the other coaches tomorrow and talk to them about this. Since they already know, we wouldn't have to explain it to them. They are so nice, and seemed to love being around kids, so I think they might give us some good tactics to use. I'm afraid if we confront Coach Sheila, she may lose her temper. I have seen her before when she looked like she was trying to keep her temper in and not let it out. It was probably because I was goofing off during practice," said Zeke with a strange look on his face. "I'm trying not to goof so much because I knew it made her mad at me when I did, and he didn't want to be on the bad side of her temper.

"Oh no, Zeke. She could have done some mean things to you too, but she must have gotten the temper under control before she did anything," said Grace with confusion. "I have an idea. Why don't we go to bed and try to get some sleep, and in the morning, we go to the other coaches when they are not around Coach Sheila and talk to them about what we might do. I don't know about you, but I'm beginning to get somewhat scared to be around her." Grace had a look of worry on her face as she explained her idea. "We need to shake off this information we found out and concentrate on the competition.

"Okay, good plan. We need to go in our bunkhouses and go to bed. Goodnight," smiled Lisa as she started walking back to their bunkhouse. Lisa was in agreement with the others about talking to the coaches. She thought that was a good plan.

Chapter Twenty-Four

Everyone went to their cots that were lower to the ground than the girls would have liked. The day had been long and tiring with swim practice and running away from strange gamblers. It put them in a state of exhaustion they hoped would improve with a good night's sleep. Tomorrow had to be a better day than what they had today.

"Grace, are you asleep?" asked Silver with a shaky voice, and her hair standing up in disarray.

"No, I can't sleep. I feel like something bad is going to happen tonight," said Grace with a strange look on her tired face. "I don't know what's going to happen, but I just have a bad feeling."

"This has been an unusual day, for sure. The good part about it was the swim practice this morning. It was fun but finding the gambling room was not. I wonder if those men that were chasing us was planning on hurting us. I think we need to be on the lookout for them," Silver said in a nervous voice. She had all the running she could handle for this trip.

Grace walked to Silver's cot, "I have an idea. Why don't we go outside and take a walk? It may make us tired enough to go to sleep."

"I like that idea. I'll get my shoes," smiled Silver who was beginning to feel better about this day and night. She was still confused at all they had seen and heard today. She was still in shock learning about their swim coach being mean. Someone that does that has to be mean to throw one of her students up against a block wall and break her hand. She hoped she didn't act nervous around coach in the morning when she saw her. That might give it away that they knew her secret, and what a secret it was, and if Coach Sheila thought they knew her secret, there is no telling what she would do to them. Silver, for sure, wasn't going to let on she knew her secret.

Grace and Silver exited the bunkhouse door and saw a trail with small lights in the ground beside it, making it easier to see here they were going. They didn't want to get lost.

Everything was going find until they heard footsteps. The girls' eyes were growing larger as the footsteps got closer. They hid behind a huge tree and glanced around often to see who it was that was walking toward them.

Chapter Twenty-Five

The gambling men, Buck and Joseph, made a plan that consisted of going to the swim camp while everyone was asleep and take the boy that was in that group of teenagers. They knew he probably wouldn't scream like one of the girls would if they were taken by strange men. After taking him, they would put him in the back room they made for storage. No one would find him there. They could let him go when everyone had gone from the swim camp. No one would ever find him.

"Buck, I think we need to go now. It's eleven o'clock. Don't you think they would all be asleep by now?" asked Joseph who wanted to get this over and done. He didn't want them to be caught for illegal gambling, but he didn't like the idea of taking one of those kids even more. Maybe they could just scare him into not saying anything and tell him he better make those girls keep their mouths shut too.

"Joseph, I think we need to wait a little longer. We need to remember these kids are teenagers and teens like to stay awake as long as they can. I don't know why they do it, they just do," explained an irritated Buck that has been this way ever since those kids saw them this afternoon. He would like to know where they went this afternoon when they ran away, because they may have already told someone, and that was something they didn't even want to think about. The police would be on their trail in no time.

"Buck, I don't like what we are going to do. We are both dads and wouldn't want one of our kids to be taken," Joseph couldn't understand how they got in this situation.

"Joseph, we don't have a choice. We'll try not to hurt him," said Buck with authority.

"Buck, look what I found," said Joseph who was proud of whatever it was.

Buck had a confused look on his scared face as he glanced at what Joseph had in his hand. "What is that? Looks like an old rag to me."

"It is a rag, but this rag is laced with chloroform," said Joseph with a smile making him look like he had just won a grand prize. Buck hated to say anything to Joseph, but he didn't like using that at all. He knew they didn't have a choice, so he would do it.

"Good idea. Perhaps we could leave now and walk slowly. Those kids swim and run around all day. They are probably all tuckered out of all their energy by this time of night. Are you ready,

Intriguing Escapade at Swim Camp

Joseph?" Buck hoped he could get Joseph to walk slowly toward the swim camp, because he wasn't too sure about using that rag to knock out a kid. What if they put too much on the rag?

"I'm ready as I'm ever going to be," laughed Joseph who was kind of enjoying this little adventure.

The happy men finally entered the park where swim campers were asleep in the bunkhouses. They didn't know which one was housing the boys, but maybe they could look in a window and could tell. They found the one where the boys slept and tiptoed slowly toward the door of the house where the boys were sleeping.

They quietly opened the squeaking door and silently went around each of the bunks until they finally found the right boy they were looking for. Joseph carefully put the rag with the chloroform over Zeke's face. The boy was sleeping so sound, he didn't make a sound or move. Maybe they didn't need the soaked rag anyway.

Buck took his arms and Joseph picked up Zeke's feet and walked out the door with him ready to take him back to the cave with them.

Chapter Twenty-Six

As the walking girls stood behind their tree wondering what was going on this late at night, they wondered who it could be. They didn't think it was the other coaches, because they would want to be up early to prepare for their practice for the day. It took some preparation on their part, and they wanted to do everything just right and be prepared for the kids to begin their drills.

"Do you think we are tired enough to go to bed and get some much-needed rest?" said Grace who was beginning to nod off at times.

"Yes, I think I am," Silver wanted to get some rest. They always do better at swimming if they had a good nights' sleep.

"STOP!" Grace whispered loudly because of what she saw.

"What is it, Grace. Did you see a snake?" Silver thought nothing was worse than a sneaky snake at night.

"Look over toward the boys' bunkhouse. What do you see?" asked Grace who wanted to know if she was seeing things.

"Oh no, I see the two men who were chasing us today from the gambling room. They are creeping along at a snail's pace. I guess they don't want to be heard. What do you think they are up too?" Silver couldn't believe those evil men were in their camp, and just what do they want inside the boys' bunkhouse?"

Grace looked at Silver, "What do you think we can do about this?"

Silver walked over to Grace and whispered, "I think we wait a few minutes until they come out and we can follow them." Grace wasn't too sure, but she wouldn't let Silver do something all by herself.

The girls waited until the door began opening and out walked the two men with a passed-out Zeke. The one named Buck was holding him under his arms, while the other one was carrying his feet. Now, the girls were really beginning to worry about what they were going to do to Zeke.

"Look, they just stopped and laid him on the ground. He must be heavy. There they go picking him up again. We need to follow them, so we can know where they are taking Zeke. They may go to the cave, but then again, they may have another place they will take him. We need to go and see. When we find out, we come back here and wake Lisa and Gold and form a plan to get him back. After swim practice, we need to do whatever we decide," said Silver who hoped their plan worked.

"Good plan, we need to follow behind them enough, so they won't see us or hear us walking. Go," whispered Grace who thought it was a good plan, and the only thing they could do right now. If they knew where they are taking him, then we can tell someone exactly where to go get him.

Grace and Silver made it without getting caught by the mean gambling men. They were taking Zeke inside the cave. They knew they couldn't go inside the cave for fear of being caught and have done to them the same thing they are doing to Zeke.

"Okay, we know where they are taking him. We need to go back and plan with Gold and Lisa," Silver was excited to have been able to see where they were taking Zeke. It will make it much easier to devise a plan. That is all they could do tonight.

Chapter Twenty-Seven

Grace and Silver turned to go back to their bunkhouse with jittery nerves, and they were jumpy at every little noise they heard. They didn't know what they would do if the men came back out and saw them. They decided they could run faster than those old men, and they probably could, considering they were in great shape from all the swimming they do to get ready for a competition, but they hoped they didn't have to try out that theory. One way or another they would rescue Zeke.

The girls who were all atwitter from their little adventure tonight of having to follow mean men who had one of their friends. They finally were nearing the camp when they saw the shadow of a person up ahead. The shadow went behind a tree to hide. Now, they were really in a bad state of mind. Who would be out this late at night and lurking around the girls' bunkhouse?" This night wasn't sitting well with the girls who followed bad men in the middle of the night.

"What do you think about that shadow up ahead?" asked Grace who thought this night was never going to be over. It was getting spookier by the minute. "It can't be anything good."

"I don't have a clue who would be out this late besides us. Of course, we have a good reason to be out here," Silver thought this whole night was getting more and more intriguing by the minute. The men have taken Zeke, and now there is a shadow, who seems to be a woman, is out hiding behind a tree watching us. They had no idea who it could be, and they weren't sure they wanted to know.

Grace looked at her friend, "That shadow is close to the door to our bunkhouse. How can we get in without being seen, and why would the shadow be there tonight? It could be a serial killer, or maybe a woman that has escaped from a mental institution. Either way, it's not good. We can't go beside whoever it is behind the tree."

"We can't go right in front of her to get inside the bunkhouse, but I just remembered there is a back door to this place. We can go around a big circle to the back door and go in that way. We need to get in there and wake Gold and Lisa, so we can concoct some sort of plan to get Zeke back," explained Silver, who was becoming jittery the closer they came to the back door. She sure hoped it wasn't locked. They didn't want to need to sleep on the hard ground outside the back door.

Intriguing Escapade at Swim Camp

Grace started laughing, "Grace, what in the world is so funny with you right now?" asked a smiling Silver. She didn't know why someone would be laughing when a friend was missing, and now a shadow of who knows what blocking their way back inside the girls' bunkhouse.

"I was wondering where you came up with a word like 'concoct'. I don't think I've ever heard that word before," laughed Grace. She knew Silver wouldn't be upset with her because she was a good friend, and she had a great sense of humor. Silver just stood still and smiled.

Silver looked her friend in the eyes and told her, "I watch a lot of TV."

Both girls heard the noise that was coming closer to where they were standing. It had to be the shadow. They didn't wait around to see what the shadow wanted, because they thought running as fast as they can toward the back door was a better plan for them at this moment.

Chapter Twenty-Eight

The running girls ran as fast as their legs would carry them to the back door with hopes it wasn't locked. They made it without incident, and lucky for them, the door was unlocked. It was sort of scary knowing they were sleeping in a bunkhouse that didn't have any of the doors locked. Anyone could come in and take someone. The more they thought about unlocked doors, the more nervous they became.

They didn't want to wake everybody, so they tiptoed to Gold and Lisa's cots and began shaking their shoulders. They both opened their sleepy eyes with a little drool running down their chin. Grace and Silver put their finger to their mouths to show them to be quiet. The girls shook their heads saying that they understood. Grace and Silver whispered for them to follow them to the corner on the right that contained a small table and some chairs. They all walked barefoot to sit at the table.

They knew they needed to whisper, so they wouldn't wake the others in the room. Grace told them about the gambling men coming to this camp and went in the boys' bunkhouse and taking

Intriguing Escapade at Swim Camp

Zeke with them. Gold and Lisa listened intently at what the girls had to say and couldn't believe the men would actually take Zeke.

"Where did they take him?" asked Lisa. "Did you follow them to make sure you knew where he might be?"

"Yes, we did follow, and they took him in the cave, but we don't know exactly where in the cave he is, but that is what we need to find out," said Silver.

"We all need to put our heads together and devise a decent plan to get him back," said Grace with authority. "Give me some of your ideas about what you think would be a good plan."

Gold raised her hand, "Gold, you don't have to raise your hand. We are not in school," smiled Grace. "What do you think we should do?"

Gold began giving them what she thinks they should do, "We need to sneak inside the cave, take our flashlights, and check everywhere in the cave. If we don't find him in the outer part of the cave, we are going to need to look inside the gambling room. They may have him tied up in there, so we need to find a knife in case they had him tied up, which I'm sure they did."

Lisa told the others she thought that might work. Grace and Silver agreed also. So, the girls made a pact to stick together when they go to the cave. No one can be away from the group. They didn't need another friend taken. Being quiet and sticking like glue to each other was the plan.

"What are we going to do if it doesn't go as planned?" Gold thought that was an essential question because it all very well could go wrong. They were praying everything would go as planned.

"I suggest we get reinforcements. We could go see if Izzy could help us. She may not can do much, but she might have some ideas, and there is Rusty, who said he would be glad to help us too. He probably would be more help than the old woman, but they would have to wait and see how it all goes down," said Grace, who liked Izzy, because she was different, and she didn't need teeth to help us. Perhaps, she could bring her tiger with her. The gambling men don't know the tiger doesn't have any teeth, and no one is afraid of a pig.

"As soon as we finish practice and put on some dry clothes, we need to meet in back of the boys' bunkhouse like last time," said Lisa, who was getting excited to go on an actual mission.

Chapter Twenty-Nine

The shadow was still standing behind a tree sulking after the girls went in the back door of the girls' bunkhouse. She needed to do something about those girls. They are the best swimmers, but not as good as her. She would have to show them who was best. She needed the perfect plan to eliminate, at least, one or two of them from being in the competition. I will take their place, then I will be the champion swimmer, and everyone would like me.

She has been reading on how to break an arm without much effort or pain on the girl. It might work to just throw them around a little, but those four girls stick like glue to each other, and there is just one of me. She will need to put more thought into this plan. These girls are champion swimmers, who should not have any problems winning their heat. The little smarties are where I wanted to be at their age, but I didn't get to do that, because my dad didn't think a girl should compete in sports, but dad is not here to stop me and her brothers wouldn't care one way or another.

Maybe I can just sit in the shadow, and it will scare them into running home to mommy. Perhaps I would not feel this way if my dear ole mom hadn't run off and left her and her brothers, and dear ole dad being abusive, but I won't use excuses.

I know I have a bad temper and should not have hurt some of the girls at her other school, but I have a therapist now, so I will not do those things anymore. I could take the girls by gunpoint somewhere and hide them, so they will not be able to complete. I would need to tie their hands and feet, and maybe hit on them a bit.

Until then, I will continue to quietly stand behind my tree every night. I know they saw me when they came back from wherever they had been. I told the parents I would take care of them and that is what I'm going to do to these little girls. I am going to take care of them alright.

"Just you wait, little darlings. Coach Sheila will give you what is coming to you. Coach Sheila will see to it that you have a good time while you are here at the camp. You just wait and see," thought the deranged coach.

Chapter Thirty

The first thing the next morning after a scary night, the teenage girls, who needed to talk to the coaches, walked over to the lake where the coaches were preparing for the swimmers' morning practice. They were all talking, laughing, and having a good time. The sun was bright as the wind blew gently making it a great day for swimming in a pretty lake.

The coaches saw the four girls walking toward them. It wasn't time for practice, but they would see what they wanted.

"Hey there, ladies. You are a little early for practice. What can we do for you?" asked Hank.

Silver smiled sweetly and said, "We have a problem, and we thought you coaches being so smart, you might help us with a problem."

"What kind of problem do you ladies have today," asked Hally with a bright smile. "We might be able to help, depending on what you need."

"Well, shall we say, we overheard you talking about Coach Sheila being fired and being mean to a girl and breaking her hand, so we went back and got on Zeke's laptop and looked her up. We are confused about what to do about it. Do we tell someone? We thought you could help us do the right thing," smiled a worried Grace. She was worried about Zeke too, but they would take care of that one themselves. The coaches just needed to help them with Coach Sheila, and how crazy she was becoming.

Dan looked at the girls, "I think you should not let Coach Sheila know that you found out about her, because it sounds like she is somewhat of a loose cannon. We don't want you hurt, and very well is what she may do."

Jaybird smiled, "You let us take care of this. It's better if we tell the appropriate people when we leave here, but whatever you do, if you see her, don't say a word about this to her. We promise we will take care of it."

"He's right, girls. You try not to let it bother you right now. You have fun and we will do the rest," said Bell with a large smile.

Chapter Thirty-One

The coaches who came to help Coach Sheila with practice and the drills, had not seen Coach Sheila in two days, and she is not in the bunkhouse. This was all confusing to them. They had been discussing what to do with the information they found about her. It's not right to keep it a secret, because that would only give her incentive to hurt someone else, and that wasn't going to happen if they could help it.

"What do you think we need to do. I think we need to tell someone before she hurts another student. It might be worse next time she does something," Jaybird couldn't imagine a coach hurting a student so bad it broke a bone, and if it continues to happen, it could be worse next time she does something like that. "We told the girls this morning that we would take care of it, so we will."

Hank looked at his brother, Jaybird, and told him he agreed with him completely. He didn't want to see another kid hurt by her hand either.

"Who do you think we need to tell?" asked Bell.

"Has anyone check this bunkhouse. She may be hiding somewhere in here and may be listening to us as we speak," said Maggie.

"She could be somewhere in here, but no one has seen her in a couple of days. She could be anywhere. Dan and Hally should search the bunkhouse while we go outside and look around," said an anxious Jaybird, who couldn't believe this was all happening, but they would take care of it soon.

"Good plan. Dan and Hally, you can start searching inside. The rest of us will go outside and spread out so we can cover more ground," Hank was just as perplexed as the rest of the coaches. They came here to help her, and now they are doing it all, which they didn't mind because it was fun, and they like to see the kids do their swimming strokes, but Coach Sheila was getting paid to do these things, and now she is gone.

"I think when we finish here at the camp, we need to go to the principal of the school, or we could go to the central office of the school system and explain what is going on and what we found out about her. I would hate to think we didn't say anything, and another kid was hurt badly," said Hally, who was becoming jittery from the thoughts of Sheila hurting another kid.

"Okay, let's do it as soon as we leave here," said Hank.

CHAPTER THIRTY-TWO

Grace, Lisa, Silver, and Gold were ready to execute their plan of rescuing Zeke from the gambling men. When they were in the cave before sneaking a peek through the crack of the door, they didn't see anyone with a gun or even a hunting knife. That was a plus, because the girls sure didn't want to be shot here at swim camp. Their parents wouldn't ever let them go anywhere again.

"I was thinking about that gambling room. There may not be many men in there in the daytime, so that would make it a little easier to get inside there. They may have another room in there where they could tie up Zeke," Silver was thinking the daytime is the best time to go in. She had no doubt that they would find Zeke in there and be able to snatch him and take him back to the camp. Even the bosses take breaks and go home for a while. It was certainly worth a try.

"We may get lucky, and no one would be in there. How cool would that be? It would be an easy in and an easy out," said Gold with a crazy smile on her face. She was as flabbergasted as the other girls, but she had confidence in all of them to feel good about what they were about to do to find Zeke. "It won't be long now, ladies before we go in the cave and come back out with Zeke in tow."

"Girls, do you think we can really do this?" asked Lisa as they slowly walked toward the cave.

"Grace, did you get the knife in case he is tied up with rope?" asked Silver who was trying to keep them all calm and make sure everything went okay. They couldn't make any mistakes.

"Yes, I have it," said Grace with a smile. When she brought the knife out of her backpack, the other girls started to run when they saw the huge knife she brought out. They had never seen a knife that big before.

"Goodness gracious, girl. Where did you get that? It's more of a weapon than a kitchen knife," Lisa was the one who was nervous at seeing such a big knife.

Grace laughed at her friends, "It's a hunting knife. My uncle has one he takes hunting with him, but I found this one under a cabinet in the kitchen. I thought it may be more efficient if the ropes are big they used to tie him." Grace thought it would surprise her friends when she got the hunting knife out of her backpack, and sure enough, they were surprised.

"We are here. Everybody, stop, and do not say a word. We will use hand signals to talk now," smiled Silver, who was enjoying this adventure a little too much. She was doing everything with a smile, while Gold and Lisa thought it was a serious mission, which it could very well be.

The girls slowly made their way to the Hobbit door and tested the knob to see if it could be opened. When they found out it was not locked, Grace twisted the knob and gently pushed it open to a small crack, so they could see if anyone was there. All the girls put their faces in the crack to see if there was anyone. When they didn't see anyone, they pushed the door open so they could get inside and search for Zeke. Since the room wasn't very big, Zeke couldn't be too hard to find.

After searching for a bit, they noticed no one was in the main room, so they would look for another door. There had to be another small room for storage to keep supplies. They began looking around for another door.

"Hey, I found another door," smiled Gold, who was proud of herself for finding the door.

The others rushed over to the door Gold found. It was locked, so Silver got a bobby pin out of her hair and tried to get it unlocked. She kept working until it finally opened. The other girls were amazed. They thought, for sure, that tactic wouldn't work.

"Girl, how did you learn to do that?" asked a confused Lisa, who really wanted to know how Silver did it.

"We have three smaller brothers who taught us, because they were always unlocking doors around the house with a bobby pin," laughed Silver.

They looked inside and saw Zeke in the floor, and he wasn't tied up. He was chained up. What do we do now? You can't cut that thick chain like you could a rope, even if you do have that gigantic knife, Grace.

"We need a new plan, girls," said Grace. "You're right. This knife is big, but it still can't cut a chain."

"Zeke, are you okay?" asked Lisa. "Don't worry. We will make another plan to get you out of here."

Zeke looked at the girls who wanted to help him, and it made him happy that someone would want to do that for him. Maybe he would stop playing so many tricks on people and be a better person.

"What do we do now?" Lisa was confused about this whole thing. "Zeke, do you have any idea when the men will be back for gambling tonight?"

"Sure. They don't start gambling until nine tonight, so if you do anything, you need to do it way before then. If you could come around six-thirty, it might still be empty in here. You might need something besides that huge knife. You could go see Rusty. I bet he would have some bolt cutters that would cut these chains." Zeke was still happy the girls cared enough to help him. He sat and smiled like he didn't have a care in the world.

"Yes, we will do that. Maybe he will come with us to help. We promise we will be back to get you, Zeke."

They all waved at Zeke and said, "Bye. See you soon. We promise."

Chapter Thirty-Three

"Okay ladies, we need to go see Miss Izzy to see what she knows about the gambling men, and if she has any ideas about helping us get Zeke out of that place. The different looks that appeared on the faces of the other girls' faces, were priceless. They ranged from worrisome to excited. They were not too sure about those animals she kept in her house. The snake was on the top of most of the girls' list of 'most scary'. The tiger didn't have any teeth, so they could deal with that.

"Wow! I like this lady. She is so funny, and you never know what she is going to say or do," said Grace with a huge smile and a giggle.

The girls arrived at Izzy's cabin, and they slowly went up on the front porch where the garlic was hanging that kept the vampires away. The cabin appeared to be in bad shape, and they weren't too sure it wouldn't fall down on them all before they left. The wood looked rotten, and the entire cabin appeared to be sagging on the right side toward the ground. They remembered, from their last visit, that the inside was not much better than the outside, but they needed to talk to Izzy, so they will take a chance.

Before the girls could knock on the door, they heard Izzy holler at them. They heard her but didn't see her anywhere. They finally looked up and saw Miss Izzy up toward the top of a huge tree. They couldn't imagine what she might be doing up so high in a tree. The girls had never seen anyone up that high in a tree before.

"What can I do for you sweet girls today?" hollered the old lady at the top of a tall oak tree.

"We have a problem you might help us with, Miss Izzy," said Silver, who really liked this old lady who liked to climb huge trees. She couldn't imagine her grandmother doing something like this.

"Come on up, and we can talk," smiled the old lady.

The girls hesitated about climbing up a tree, but they finally jumped on a short limb, so they could go closer to Izzy. They wouldn't go up as high as she was, but they would get high enough to hear what she had to say about their situation.

"Okay, young ladies, tell me what you have on your mind," smiled Izzy as she watched the girls slowly climb the big tree. Miss Izzy figured the girls didn't have as much experience climbing trees as she had.

"The mean gambling men have taken our friend, Zeke, who was with us when we saw you last time. We need to know if you have any ideas, or could you help us get him back," explained Grace with sincerity.

"We need to hop down out of the tree and go sit in the kitchen, so we can talk better," smiled the old lady. The girls were amazed that she was out of the tree before they were, but like she said, Izzy had more experience.

The excited girls slowly got off their limb and when they got farther down, they jumped out of the tree. Little old lady jumped from where she was high up in the old tree. When she landed, she rolled like a snowball all the way down the hill. The girls didn't know whether to laugh or cry. They chose to laugh.

They all made it to the kitchen and took a seat at the long table, "I have been pondering over your situation and have come up with an idea. We could take the snake, tiger, pig, cat, and the monkey and let them lose in the gambling room, and they should destroy the whole room and while they are doing that, we get Zeke and take him out of there."

The girls weren't too sure about that plan, but they didn't want to hurt Izzy's feelings, so they agreed. They told her they were going to go to visit Rusty and see if he has bolt cutters.

Intriguing Escapade at Swim Camp

"Okay. Bring Rusty with you and come back by here to get me and the animals. This should do the trick," smiled old lady.

Chapter Thirty-Four

Grace, Lisa, Silver, and Gold, and Izzy trotted toward Rusty's house to borrow some bolt cutters. The girls thought they were making things happen now. They were excited they would be able to rescue Zeke from the horrible gambling men. It was fortunate for them that they were able to talk to Zeke, so he could fill them in about when the other men came to gamble. He told them that Buck and Joseph left, but they didn't tell him where they were going, so Zeke couldn't say when they would be returning.

They all walked to Rusty's door, and a pretty woman that was singing opened it and told them to come right in after she got the grace out of *Amazing Grace*. "Rusty, we have company." Ruby liked when company came. They lived so far away from everything they didn't have people come by too often.

"Hey ladies, it's good to see you again." Rusty hugged Izzy, who just happened to be his grandmother. That was sort of a shocker to the teenage girls.

The girls began to tell Rusty what was happening with Zeke being taken by the gambling men, and that they needed bolt cutters

Intriguing Escapade at Swim Camp

to release him. Rusty couldn't believe two grown men would kidnap a teenage boy. That was beyond horrible to Rusty. He would get his bolt cutters and go with the kids.

"I'll help you get Zeke out of the clutches of the gambling men. I don't know any of them, but it wasn't right to kidnap a teenager," said Rusty. "I want to introduce you girls to my family. We have ten children and six of these are twins. Yes, we had three sets of twins. Over in the righthand corner are Bobbie and Robbie. To your left, is Tonya and Sonya, and they are beside Will and Bill. The other kids are not twins. They are Maggie, Susie, Tommy, and Faith, and, last but not least, is my beautiful wife of sixteen years, Ruby. Ruby gave the girls a huge smile.

The girls all smiled and said hi to Rusty's family. Ruby, who had been listening to what the girls were talking about, went over to Rusty and said, "Rusty, you have to help these girls. It's the right thing to do."

"Yes, ma'am, I sure will help them," said Rusty as he smiled at his sweet wife.

"Mother, I shouldn't be too long. I'll be back soon. You kids be good and mind your mama," said Rusty as they went out the door.

"I supposed Grandma has all her animal friends with her outside, and I have bolt cutters. Those animals should tear that place up, which is what needs to be done," said Rusty, who couldn't wait to see what Izzy's animals did to the gambling room.

The menagerie of people and animals walked toward the cave on a rescue mission. They found the cave without any effort and walked toward the opening. After going inside, they went straight to the Hobbit door. Rusty pushed the door open with a loud slam against the wall. Buck and Joseph ran toward them, and that is when Izzy let her animals loose in the room. Buck and Joseph ran to the back of the room and watched as all the animals knocked over tables and chairs and even broke a few of them. The disgruntled gambling men stood silently watching what they had made being torn to pieces.

"Make them stop," hollered Buck, who couldn't believe what he was seeing. He couldn't imagine why someone would have a tiger and a monkey, much less a large snake. They saw the old toothless woman laughing at what her babies was doing to the men's gambling room.

Rusty raised his bolt cutters and said, "The only way we make it stop is for you to take us to where the boy is you took from the swim camp. If not, the animals stay and play cards with you."

"Okay," said Buck as he pointed toward the storage room door. Rusty and his bolt cutters walked over to the storage room and used his cutters to free Zeke. Zeke was never so happy in his life to get free of these insane men. He ran over and hugged all the girls and shook Rusty's hand. This day turned out good for Zeke. He was thankful to all who helped the girls rescue him from these mean men.

The gambling men promised they would not take any more kids. That's when the police walked in behind the others. They got handcuffs off their belts and put them on Buck and Joseph. They were being arrested for illegal gambling and kidnapping.

Before the police left the gambling room, the one named Eli looked at Miss Izzy, "Izzy, you need to collect your animals and go home now. Thanks for helping the boy that was taken."

The kids thanked Rusty and Izzy and went on their way back to the camp with a promise to go see Rusty and Izzy again before they leave to go home.

"Wow! What a day this has been," said a laughing Grace. "But it has turned out well since they were able to rescue Zeke back."

Chapter Thirty-Five

Coach Sheila begins searching for Grace and her friends. She knew they went to the zipline every day, so that would be the first place she will go. They are not going to steal my thunder. I will be the championship swimmer as soon as I take these giggly girls and hide them where no one can find them. People just don't understand me, and that's their fault. I'm not really a bad person. I have a bit of a temper at times, but her therapist is helping with that, and soon I will be good as gold.

She heard the other coaches talking about her. They didn't know she was behind a tree, and she heard every word they said. They were not going to tell the ones in charge of the teacher about what she did in the past to other students. She didn't really want to hurt them, but they asked for it, so she had to dole out the punishment. Sheila wondered why kids didn't always listen to the adults. I only say things one time, and they need to listen when I say it the first time. She had learned that the hard way from her dad. He could really dole out the punishment, and he taught me everything I know about that.

Intriguing Escapade at Swim Camp

When I take the girls and hide them, I am going to tell the coaches that no one will know where they are unless they promise not to tell the principal about her past. Then I will think about letting them know where the girls are being kept. That may be my only chance of no one knowing her secret except her and her therapist. They won't outsmart me.

She made it to the zipline and looked around to find Grace, Lisa, Silver, and Gold. She noticed Zeke Sheet hanging around the girls a lot, also. So, if she finds the girls, she will most likely find Zeke too. After searching the entire zipline area, she didn't see the girls or Zeke anywhere. Oh great, they decided not to zipline today. They go every day. She wondered why they didn't make it today. They still may come later this afternoon. She would try to wait patiently.

"I have a good idea. I can sabotage the zipline cable, so it will be weaker and not hold up the girls. That would take care of at least one of them, if not more," thought Sheila with a sneaky smile. Now she was thinking better. The coaches wouldn't be telling anyone anything today.

Sheila's heart went down in her stomach when late afternoon came, and they got the news that the zipline cable broke and a boy fell off and broke his leg. Sheila knew if anyone saw her, she would be in bad trouble. Perhaps when she finds the group she had been hunting for and hides them, she will leave the park and go far away. If she doesn't leave, then she may be in more trouble than she had ever been in before.

Chapter Thirty-Six

The men who control the zipline couldn't understand how this had happened. They check every inch of the zipline before letting anyone on. It shouldn't have happened to the boy. They felt bad, but they had done their job of inspecting it. Two of the men went to check everything again to see if they could find out what went wrong. They felt so bad the boy was hurt. They would do all they could to find what the problem was. It wouldn't fix the boy's leg, but they could fix it so no one else would be harmed again.

They searched and searched and finally found something jammed in a place that only a person could have done. They didn't want to accuse anyone, but that was the only way this could have happened. We need to snap a picture of this and go show it to the boss. He will be livid this had happened, but he was a reasonable man and would know the workers didn't have anything to do with this. The boss knows all his workers and trusts them. It had to be someone else, but who in their right mind would do this to a bunch of kids or ever adults? It had to be someone who was deranged to put kids in danger.

The men who had found the problem fixed it, and one of them went down the zipline to make sure it was fixed. It was fixed, but they still closed it down for the rest of the day. Even though it wasn't the fault of the zipline people, they were still afraid of a lawsuit. Maybe they could find the person who did this, and they would be off the hook. They would get started talking to the people. Someone had to see something.

The boss didn't want anything else to happen, so he made the decision to close it the rest of the week. He knew they kids here loved to do it every day, but it couldn't be helped. He didn't want any more kids being hurt. He didn't think the swim people wouldn't be here much longer either. He was content with his decision to close the zipline for now.

The workers agreed with the boss. They were all still in shock at someone trying to do something like this to these kids. They were going to look around and ask everyone who was staying at the swim camp if they saw anyone messing around with anything on the zipline. Surely, someone had to have seen who did it. There are people walking around here at the camp all the time.

CHAPTER THIRTY-SEVEN

The girls, who had rescued Zeke, were ambling back toward the swim camp singing all the way. They were happy they could be a part of rescuing their friend and were glad he was back with them. He was fun to be around, and the girls knew he really liked them, and would help them do things. It never hurt to have a boy in their group. The girls knew Zeke would make a good friend.

As they walked, Grace, who liked pretty flowers, decided their bunkhouse could use some of those she saw while they were going back. "Hey, I'm going to pick some of those flowers to spruce up our bunkhouse. I won't be long, so I'll catch up with you in a bit. I won't pick too many."

"Go ahead, girl. Our bunkhouse could use some color," said Silver who liked pretty flowers.

After around ten minutes, Zeke and the girls decided they would help Grace with those flowers, so they turned around to go help, and they stopped completely still without saying a word. Apparently, Grace had picked a bunch of flowers, but they had been dropped and were all over the ground. Grace was nowhere to be seen. The girls began to get worried, since they knew Grace wouldn't go anywhere else without telling them. She was extremely considerate of everyone.

"Someone had to take Grace. She wouldn't just run away. That's not like her," said Lisa who was beginning to worry.

Zeke and the girls' minds were jostled as to where she could have gone. There weren't any houses or buildings in this area for her to go to, and they didn't think she would do that anyway. Perhaps they should sit on the ground and wait a while because she may come back from where she went, but they didn't really think that, because she wouldn't pick flowers, and then throw them on the ground. She was taken.

"I don't know about you ladies, but I'm getting a bit hungry," said Zeke, who was a boy and apparently boys had to eat more often than girls.

"It's not time to eat dinner yet. You will have to wait like us. We are patient, and you are not," said Silver, who was a touch irritated that Grace hasn't been seen yet. It wasn't like her to do something like this. "She wouldn't have a reason to run away. She has been taken."

****

Intriguing Escapade at Swim Camp

Sheila knew she shouldn't have taken Grace, but she was going to stick to her plan. She got lucky when she saw Grace picking flowers, so she took her piece of cloth to put over Grace's face, so she could grab her and take her to the old barn she found near the swim camp. No one would think to look there for her. She thought her plan was taking form. All she needs now were the other girls that make up the clique.

She felt good when she grabbed Grace. She would get the others, but she had to take them one at a time unless she could get her hands on a gun, so she could bring them in at gunpoint. After she tied Grace to a post, she looked around. Sheila couldn't find anything, but she remembered she had a candy bar in her pocket. She could put it in one of the girls back and the others would think she had a gun and go with her. She hoped that would work. If not, she would need to use a different strategy.

Silver had sat as long as she wanted to. She was somewhat hyper and couldn't sit for long periods of time. She told the others she was going back to look for Grace, or at least see if she could find some clues to where she may have gone.

The others agreed and said they would still be here when she got back. They would all go, but it didn't take this many people to get one girl. They told Silver they would get some rest while she was gone. It had been a long day, and it wasn't over yet. They wouldn't go back to camp until they found their friend.

Sheila walked out of the barn and in the small distance, she saw Silver walking that way. She got her cloth to put over her face. This was her lucky day. She grabbed Silver after putting the cloth over her face to keep her from yelling and tied her to another post next to Grace. Silver tried to fight, but Coach Sheila was strong.

Sheila didn't know if she could be lucky enough for the rest of them to start this way, but when she went out, she saw three kids walking her way. She knew she couldn't get all of them, so she would make another plan. She ran up to the three kids and said, "Come quickly, Grace and Silver are hurt. They are in a barn over the hill."

The kids began running to help their other two girls. When they went in the barn, they noticed they were tied to a post and were sitting in the hay on the floor. Sheila quickly stuck her candy bar in the back of Gold making her lose her breath, and her eyes go bigger as coach held her with a gun.

"Don't say a word, or I will shoot Gold. Do as I say. Zeke, get the rope beside the door and tie Lisa to a post. If you try anything, I will shoot her. I swear I will," smiled an elated Coach Sheila. Everything was going her way right now. Perhaps things would be going her way for a while and give her time to run far away where no one would ever find her. She thought her plan was working for her.

"I'm going to take Gold to a post, so Zeke can tie her, then I want Zeke to go back to camp and tell the other coaches that I have the girls, but I will let them go if they promise not to tell the principal about my past. I know they found out, but I will not go down without a fight. If they tell, no one will ever hire me again. I will be destitute." The kids stared at their coach, who at the moment, they thought was crazy.

"Coach Sheila, why do you hurt kids?" asked a stressed Gold, who could not believe this was happening. They didn't know what coach Sheila was going to do next. Was she going to kill them, or just leave them here for no one to find them?

"Shut up, you, little goofball." That's when she slapped Gold across her face making Silver squirm around trying to get the ropes off her. If she could get loose, she would get Sheila and perhaps tie Coach to a post. Silver went ballistic when she saw Coach Sheila slap her sister.

Coach Sheila looked at Zeke, "Go on and tell them what I said, boy."

Chapter Thirty-Eight

Clay and Josh couldn't imagine why anyone would do such a horrible thing as messing with the cables of a zipline. They felt sorry for the boy who fell and broke his leg. He was probably lucky, because he could have been killed if he had landed on his head instead of his leg. The boss wants them to walk around and talk to people to see if they saw anyone going to the zipline when it wasn't open yet. As many people who are here, someone had to see something. They would need to try to talk to as many people as they can.

"Clay, I sure hope we find someone who knows who did this. It makes me sad for the poor boy who broke his leg," said Josh, who had a boy the age of the one who fell, and he couldn't imagine what the parents were going through. It was a horrible feeling to have someone call you and tell you his kid fell off a zipline and broke his leg. If it was Clay, he would be devastated if it had been his son.

"I know. The boss said if we find anyone, he is going to call the police to come get them, and I don't blame him. They need to be punished," Clay thinks if the police don't come, he will get that person and tie them up and take them to the police. What was done to the zipline was a horrible act to do and they needed to be punished.

"I see some a couple of men up to the left by one of the bunkhouses. Let's go talk to them first. I noticed them before. They are outside a lot, especially when the kids are practicing their swimming. They may be coaches," said Clay.

"Hi, I'm Clay and this is Josh." They shook the hands of the two men. "We work at the zipline and are talking to people to see if they have noticed anyone that looked suspicious going to the zipline when it was closed."

"We heard about that. It was sad the boy broke his leg, but it could have been worse," said Jaybird, who told the zipline men they were helping coach the swimmers. "I didn't see anyone, but there are many people out here occasionally. We will ask people we see and will definitely let you now if we find out anything.

"I saw a man walking toward the zipline one day, but he turned around when he got halfway way and came back. I guess he noticed it wasn't open yet. He wouldn't have had time to do damage to the zipline though," explained Hank.

"Thanks. If you think of anyone else, please let us know," smiled Josh. "It was nice to meet you."

"They came upon a woman who was sitting around a firepit that wasn't lit, and she told them she saw a woman who was walking that way, and she was gone for quite a while," said the firepit woman, who was glad she could help. She heard about the boy who fell off and broke his leg. She couldn't understand how someone could do that to a kid.

"Did you know her, ma'am?" asked Clay, who was getting a bit antsy because they had not had any luck so far. They didn't know if this woman could help them or not.

"No," said firepit lady.

"Could you describe what she looked like, ma'am?" asked Josh, who was beginning to think this woman couldn't help them.

"Yes, she had short curly blond hair and a whistle around her neck. I remember the whistle because I thought it was strange for a woman to walk around with a whistle around her neck.

"Thank you, ma'am," said Josh with a smile.

Clay and Josh walked back over to the swim coaches they talked to earlier, because they knew they might know her since they had a whistle around their necks too.

"Hi, Jaybird, a lady told us she saw a lady walk that way and was gone quite a while. She described her as having short curly blond hair and a whistle around her neck. Would she happen to be in your group?" asked Clay, who thought they might be getting somewhere now.

Hank looked at the two men, "That sounds like it could be Coach Sheila. I don't know her last name, but she should still be here somewhere. I haven't seen her in a long while, but if I do, I'll let you know."

"Thank you, gentlemen."

Chapter Thirty-Nine

Jaybird and Hank found the rest of the coaches and began talking about what the two men from the zipline found out. They didn't know how anyone could do such a thing. That boy could have been hurt worse than a broken leg. It made them cringe to think it could have been one of their group that was hurt.

"That's it. We need to tell what we know about Coach Sheila. The way the woman described her was exactly like her characteristics. It had to have been her that sabotaged the zipline. Apparently, Miss Sheila does not have a conscious about hurting people," said Bell, who couldn't believe she would do that. None of the coaches could believe Sheila would do such a thing as harming anyone, and especially, a kid. She has to be insane. Something has to be done with her and soon.

"Why don't we try to find her? I don't think telling her what we know about her would help, because she might hurt us all. We keep the secret until we leave this place, or one of us could go to the school and talk to the principal and tell it all," explained Jaybird who wanted this all over.

Intriguing Escapade at Swim Camp

"Do you think the principal would be at the school now?" asked Maggie, who was having a hard time believing anyone would try to hurt kids. No one in their right mind would hurt a child.

"It seems like principals are always at the school. They are on a twelve-month contract. They even have to work during the summer," smiled Hank who knew this for a fact, since his mom had been a principal before she retired.

Dan looked at the other coaches and said, "I think we need to go to the zipline and talk to the men and tell them who did this. They would probably call the police, as they should. That way it is out of our hands except for telling the principal, and I'm sure the principal would need to go tell the superintendent.

"That makes sense. I think Jaybird should go talk to the principal, and Hank and Dan will go tell the zipline people." They were sure the boss of the zipline would call the police because that made them look bad.

When Jaybird gave him all the information they knew about Coach Sheila, the principal was beginning to become somewhat angry. He wanted Jaybird to help him find where he found the information about her online, so he could see it for himself. He was appalled when he read about her. He couldn't understand why they didn't know this before she was hired. Surely, the PR person in the central office called the school where she came from for a reference.

"Thank you so much for letting me know about this. I will need to go to our central office today and explain it to the superintendent," said the disgruntled principal, who was wondering how she got by all this when they called her references. She may have paid people to give her a good recommendation.

"You're welcomed. We couldn't not tell you because it's kids we are talking about, and kids matter," said Jaybird who was glad to get this off his chest. It had been bothering him and the other coaches ever since they found out about Coach Sheila. They knew they had to tell, or they wouldn't be able to live with themselves if they hadn't. What if she hurts another kid before anything is done about her?

Jaybird could only imagine what the parents would think or say about all this. He knew if it had been his kids that were involved with her, his wife and him would not like it at all. Coach Sheila needs to be in jail. There is no excuse for doing what she has done to kids, and he didn't think she should be allowed to be around kids anymore.

The other coaches were parents also, and he knew they would be just as upset as he was. It had been a horrible experience knowing what they knew about the coach, but it was good to get it off their chest, so they could go back to thinking about the next practice. They would do whatever they needed to for the kids. Their kids were good swimmers and seemed to get better every day.

"Perhaps if the police become involved, it will all be over soon. They will get another coach. If they can't find one before the competition, then Jaybird, Hank, and Dan will volunteer to help until they can find another coach.

CHAPTER FORTY

Jason had returned to the swim camp and told what he had told the principal, and what the principal said he was going to do. This should take care of it. The others were glad they had told someone because it made them feel better. They sure didn't want her to hurt another kid. They felt sorry for the parents of the little boy who was hurt with a broken leg because of her. They knew if the boy's parents find out who did that atrocious act, they will probably want to sue, or, at least take her to court.

"I think someone needs to volunteer to be coaches in case they can't find someone before the competition." They all agreed and said they would love to do it. It would bring back memories of the swimming competition days. After all, they knew what they were doing to help the swimmers to do their best. They had noticed the kids were making progress since they came to the camp. They were proud of the kids, because they have worked hard to be better for the competition.

"Has anyone seen our dear ole Coach Sheila lately. I don't believe I have seen her for a couple of days. Where do you think she could be?" asked Maggie. "She may still be here but is hiding. I don't know where someone could hide in a place like this.

"Perhaps we should search around the camp and see if we can find her. She may know we found out about her and is in hiding. She should be ashamed of what she has done, but people like that don't have a shameful bone in their body," said Dan who was glad she wasn't his coach when he was doing competitions. They didn't have sympathy for someone who did things to kids like she has done here and at the other places she has worked. They deserve whatever they get when they go to trial.

The coaches searched and searched and even asked some of the kids if they had seen her, but no one had for a couple of days. The only one who has seen her lately was the firepit woman who saw her go to the zipline. They found that same woman and asked her a few more questions. They hoped she wouldn't mind, but they needed to know.

"Ma'am, could we ask a few questions about the woman you saw going to the zipline area?" asked Hally with a sweet smile.

"I guess I can. What do you need to know?" asked the smiling lady.

"Do you remember what kind of clothes she was wearing?" asked Hally, who was all about clothes and knew all the brand names.

"Well, let's see," said the lady as she appeared to be thinking as she put her pointing finger on her cheek.

"She had on black shorts that I thought was way too short, but that's just me. I remember she had on a blue shirt that said something about swimming on it," she smiled at the coaches because she liked helping people. "It was awful about that little boy falling off the zipline, wasn't it? Are you thinking this woman I saw may be the one who broke the zipline? I don't know about those ziplines. I think if God wanted us to fly, He would have given us wings.

"Yes, ma'am, it was terrible about the boy," said Hank. "Thank you, ma'am. That was helpful. You have a blessed day."

The coaches turned around to go back to the bunkhouses and search one more time, until they heard a voice calling for them. It was Zeke, and he was running fast toward them and had a look of fear on his face. They stopped and let Zeke catch up to them. This couldn't be good, and the coaches had a bad feeling about this. The boy must have run quite a way to be so give out. He is a swimmer and in good shape.

Intriguing Escapade at Swim Camp

Before saying anything, Zeke had to bend over to catch his breath from running so hard, "Coach, you have to help. Coach Sheila has gone off the deep end, and has tied Grace, Lisa, Silver, and Gold to a post in an old barn. She may kill them. I don't know. She told me to tell you something." He was talking so vigorously the others were having trouble hearing him and told him to calm down, so they could understand what he was trying to tell them.

"Whoa, there boy. Calm down and talk a little slower. Did you say that Coach Sheila has the girls tied up to a post in an old barn?" asked Dan with a serious expression. "Why did she do that? Did she give a reason for tying the girls to a post?"

"Yes, she made me tie them up to the post and then told me to tell you that she will release them if you promise not to tell anyone about her past. Oh yeah, Grace and Silver had a huge bruise on one of their legs, and Gold and Lisa had a huge bruise on their face." Zeke was still upset and hyper that she had done these things to his friends. He hoped he could still be their friend. It was Coach who made him tic the girls to a post.

"Are you going to help?" asked a nervous Zeke who wanted to do the right thing for the girls.

"Yes, we are, Zeke, but first we are going to need to discuss this. We can't just run in willie-nillie without some sort of plan of what would be the best thing to do.

Chapter Forty-One

The coaches stood completely still as they listened to everything Zeke had told them to say to them. They knew they had to do something before she hurt the girls any more than she already has. They couldn't believe all this was happening. Yesterday, they were coaching kids at swimming and now some of the girls have been taken by a crazy lady. They knew they had to do something before they were hurt again.

"Zeke, you can go with us, so you can lead us to the barn," said Hank as he patted Zeke on the back. He knew Zeke was still shivering and thought he should try to calm him so he could help them find the barn. Hank knew he was friends with the girls and was upset that Coach Sheila made him tie the girls to the posts. They couldn't understand why Coach would do that.

Dan looked at Hank and Zeke standing appearing to be deep in thought, "We go up to the outside of the barn door, but we would need to be in complete silence. If Sheila thought we were out there, she might do something else to the girls."

Intriguing Escapade at Swim Camp

"Zeke, did Coach Sheila have any kind of weapon with her?" asked Maggie, who softly whispered something to Bell.

Zeke looked at the others, "She said she had a gun and put in Gold's back and said if I didn't tie up the girls, she would shoot Gold, but when I looked back at Coach, it didn't look like a gun. It may have been a candy bar, but I'm not sure." The coaches were mad because of what Coach Sheila was putting them through. It might take them a few days to get the girls and Zeke back on track with their swimming because of being upset over all this horrible thing that has happened to them.

"If she had a real gun, that would be even more trouble for her," said Hally.

"When she took these girls, it made her add kidnapping to her list of crimes, and if she has a real gun, then that guarantees her a cell in the state prison," said Hank.

"Okay, in ten minutes, we go toward the barn. As soon as we get in sight of the barn, we start walking slowly and we can't make a sound. We go up to the door and listen first, then we charge in. Jaybird will go in first and the lady coaches can take care of taking down Sheila and grab her while the others untie the girls. Then we tie up Sheila and take her to the police," said Maggie. If we are lucky, the police will make it there before we have to do much.

They heard a noise of men talking and turned around and saw the police with the zipline men coming toward the coaches. Thank goodness, they could take over now. They knew how to do these things.

Chapter Forty-Two

Sheila walked in front of the girls she had tied to posts. She didn't say a word, she just walked in front of them with a smirk on her face. The girls didn't know what she had planned, but they didn't like it that she didn't say anything to them. They couldn't even begin to imagine what she was thinking, or maybe they didn't need to know what she had planned for them. Whatever it was, they were sure they wouldn't like it.

Grace looked over at the other girls. Gold had tears in her eyes, and Lisa sat staring at the hay on the floor. Silver was like Grace. They both had looks of intense anger on their dirty faces and looked like steam was about to float out of their ears. They didn't know why Coach Sheila was doing this, but there was absolutely no reason she could think of for her to be so mean to them. They had always done their best for her, and this is how she repays us by tying us to a post and make bruises on us. The woman was looney.

Grace, without anything to do, began looking around their surroundings. There might be something they could use to untie their hands. The old barn didn't look like it had been used lately.

There were a few bales of hay up in the loft, but the hay that had fallen on the floor looked old like it had been there for a while. She didn't see any tools hanging on the walls, or not a shovel or a hoe in sight. So much for freeing themselves from the ropes she made Zeke put on us. They worried about Zeke. They knew he would do what she told him to do, but they didn't want him to get in trouble with Sheila or anyone else. One thing they did know was that Zeke would be one of the ones coming to rescue them.

Grace knew Silver could help her if they can find a way to get out of here, but Gold and Lisa were not able to do anything, because they were so devastated about what was happening to them. It saddened Grace and Silver when they saw the huge bruise on the cheeks of the other two girls.

Silver looked at Coach and asked, "Can you tell us why we are being treated like animals?" Silver didn't know if she should have asked Coach anything or not, since she hasn't talked to them in quite a while, but Silver didn't care. Someone had to say something. She would say something, because she could take almost anything Coach could dish out to them.

"It's really none of your business what I do or say, so shut up," Sheila couldn't believe Silver and Grace weren't as upset as the other two girls. What was wrong with them? Those two were definitely braver than the other two. They must not think she will do anything to them. Maybe she should show them different.

"Why aren't you two squirts upset like Gold and Lisa? Are you crazy?" asked Coach, who wanted to run away and get this day over and done. What is wrong with Grace and Silver that they are not afraid of me.

"I think you are the one that is crazy," stated Grace who was waiting for Sheila's temper to erupt. Grace thought that if she made Coach mad, she might make some mistakes and they could free themselves. That was the only thing she could think of at the moment.

Silver whispered to Grace, "You go girl. Good job."

"No, I'm not crazy, and you better watch your mouth, little girl. Why aren't you and Silver not upset?" asked the crazy coach who was confused as to why the girls weren't afraid of her. All the kids need to be afraid of me.

"We prayed, and we believe Jesus will take care of us," said Grace with a mammoth smile. Sheila didn't like her smile at all, so she hit her again on the other cheek. Grace didn't cry. She just smiled at the one who hit her again.

"You have got to be kidding me? No one can help you now, because no one knows where you are, so shut up." Sheila was talking viciously making Gold and Lisa become more terrified.

Silver and Grace sat smiling at coach Sheila making Coach even more enraged. The girls thought she might explode at any minute. She walked over to the girls and kicked Grace and Silver on the other leg, and then proceeded to go to Gold and Lisa and punched them in the face for not being alert.

"You didn't have to do that. What were they doing to you? Nothing, absolutely nothing. You are a horrible person who has no heart," said Silver who wanted to say more, but she didn't want to enrage her even more. "What has been done to you to make you so mean?"

"You need to be quiet. You don't know anything. Did you live with a dad who beat you all the time or have brothers who had to take care of you after your mother left when you were young? I don't think so," said Sheila as she looked at the girls with contempt.

"That's bad, but it's not worth getting into trouble over, and you will get in trouble for all you have done to kids. I know you didn't have a good home life, but that's no excuse for the things you have done. You should strive to be better and have a happy life. I don't believe you are a happy person," said Grace with a smile. "You can overcome all that. Why don't you come with me and Silver to church this Sunday? Jesus loves you, you know."

Intriguing Escapade at Swim Camp

"What are you going to do? Pray for me?" asked the disgruntled coach, who couldn't believe she was talking about religion with these brats.

"Yes, ma'am. I will," said Grace with the same smile. "You have to have some good in you somewhere."

Grace looked at Silver and whispered to her, "If she comes by our post, if we can, we should stick our feet out when she walks over and trip her."

Chapter Forty-Three

The coaches couldn't believe they were having to devise a plan to rescue some of the girls here at the camp. They just came to help with practice, but it has turned into something entirely different. They knew they wouldn't let the girls stay in that barn tied to a post, but they needed to do it right. They would do what they could to help the girls be free of an insane woman swimming coach.

"Zeke, you need to go back and tell Coach Sheila we have a deal. We won't tell, and she unties the girls and will let them come back to the camp," Hank knew Zeke was concerned about the girls, and he wanted to help. "Then you come back and let us know what's going on in the barn."

"Okay, Coach, I'll be back as fast as I can run," smiled Zeke who was happy to help his new friends.

After Zeke left the building, the coaches began to talk. "For some reason, I don't think Sheila will let the girls come back with Zeke. She is not that kind of person. If she doesn't, we need to go in there and get the girls, and we tie Sheila to a post until the police can come get her," said Bell. "I know, for a fact, the zipline boss has already called the police."

"That's a good idea. We go in if she doesn't let them come back. I like that. There are six of us and only one of her. Surely, we can get her and tie her to a post. I think the three girls in our group could go inside the barn and overtake Sheila. Hold her down until we can get her tied up.

What the coaches didn't know was that Zeke went to visit Izzy, and she will be coming with her group of exotic animals to guard Coach Sheila, so she won't get any ideas of trying to escape. The coaches should be pleasantly surprised about that.

Chapter Forty-Four

Jaybird's cell phone began vibrating in his pocket while he was with the other coaches. They had made their plan and felt good about it. He answered his phone, and when he ended the call, he told the others about it. "That was the principal, who is now at the central office, and he wants me to come tell the superintendent all that I know about Coach Sheila."

"I guess she will lose her job. She needs to do something except be around kids," said Maggie.

"Do you know where she was before this job?" asked Bell, who was curious about why she left.

"I think I know why she left," said Dan. "I read all about her too, and she was fired from the last job when she threw a girl against a block wall breaking her hand. Personally, I think they should have put her in jail for child abuse right then, but they just fired her and now she is being mean to kids here too."

Jaybird came back from the central office where the principal and the superintendent were discussing what to do to Sheila, along with being fired from her job. They didn't know how they missed her past when they were calling the references she gave them when she applied for this job. She must have gotten friends to be the references, so they would give her a good one. Someone missed calling the school she was at before here. If they had known about her, she never would have had a job here. When they talked about her throwing a girl against a block wall, they all began shaking their head.

"The superintendent said this was a lesson learned, and it wouldn't be happening again. He would be explaining this at the next meeting with his staff. When I told him about what she had done now by taking four girls and tying them in a barn, they were devastated," said Jaybird.

CHAPTER FORTY-FIVE

Zeke wanted to help but didn't know exactly what to do. He knew the grown-ups would take care of getting the girls back and tying up Coach Sheila, but he would need to help too, because the girls that are tied to a post are his friends, and friends help each other. He wanted to be a good friend. They did the same for him when the gambling men took him and chained him. He would do what he had to do for the girls. He didn't like it when he saw bruises on the girls.

Zeke thought and thought about what he could do for his part of rescuing the girls. He might get a huge stick and threaten his coach if she didn't untie the girls, or maybe he could go with the grown-ups and help them. His weapon could be the big stick. He didn't know why Coach Sheila did these things, but it wasn't right. Maybe a port-a-potty fell on her head when she was a little girl and now has brain damage. He didn't know for sure what made people do bad things. He tried not to do bad things. He always like to prank people, but he didn't think that was too bad.

Intriguing Escapade at Swim Camp

Zeke began thinking again, "If I had a dad, I know he would have taught me how to fight, but since I don't, I will just have to make do and teach myself. You can look up anything on the internet, so I could do that. Another idea is to find a way on the outside of the barn to climb up into the loft, and maybe I would get a chance to untie the girls, and no one would know how I got inside." Zeke's mind was going round and round as he thought of different scenarios to help the girls.

When he thought of climbing up in the loft from the outside, he thought of Miss Izzy and how she shimmies up a tree, but there are no limbs on a barn. I've got it. I will go see Miss Izzy and see what she thinks I should do. I like her. She is so fun to be around.

Zeke walked to the cabin with the garlic hanging on the porch and knocked on her door. Miss Izzy came to the door and when she saw Zeke, she began to smile. "Come on in here, Zeke," said a happy Izzy. Apparently, she didn't get much company. She was happy when these kids came to see her. "Where are the girls?"

"Sit down at the table. We were just starting to have our snack for the day," said Izzy with that same silly grin on her face. Zeke sat down in a chair beside Mikey, the monkey. In the other chairs was Oink, Witchy, Sneaky, and Tigger. Zeke thought these animals were so cool.

He proceeded to tell Miss Izzy about the situation with the girls who were here with last time. She was upset this had happened to the girls, so she told Zeke that when the other coaches went to get the girls out and tie up Coach Sheila, she would go with them and let her animals be the ones to watch over Coach Sheila, so she won't try to run away when the police come for her.

Zeke left Miss Izzy's house feeling much better now that he had done something to help. He could go back now and feel good. He couldn't wait to see the girls and see if they were okay.

Chapter Forty-Six

The coaches talked about it, and they decided to go rescue the girls in an hour. They would need to see if they need anything to take with them. They thought taking the first aid kit might be a good idea. They didn't know what all Coach Sheila had done to the girls. They shouldn't need any weapons. They thought between all six of them, they could surely overpower her.

After eating their meal of hotdogs and chips, they decided it was time to go do this before it got dark, because they knew the barn probably didn't have any lights if it was as old as Zeke said it looked like it was. Bell put some snacks and apple juice in a bag to take to the girls who haven't eaten in quite a while. She knew someone who ties up kids is not going to feed them, and if she did, it wouldn't be much. Bell knew how much teenagers ate, so she would take food and drink.

"Okay, ladies and gentlemen, are we ready to go to the rescue of the four girls and take down a swim coach?" laughed Hank as he walked toward the bunkhouse door. Zeke will be going with them to show them the way to the old barn.

"Zeke, was there any animals in the barn when you were in there?" asked Jaybird, who didn't particularly want to step in a pile of poop while rescuing the girls.

"No, I didn't see any," Zeke laughed because he knew there would be animals, because he had asked Izzy to bring hers so they could stand guard over Coach Sheila.

The group of coaches followed Zeke as he led them to the barn where the girls were being held. They thanked Zeke for getting them to the right place.

"It's right over this next hill," said Zeke.

"Okay, lead the way," smiled Dan.

They stopped at the door before going inside. Suddenly, they heard the screaming of the girls.

"Oh no, she's killing them," said Zeke.

They all burst inside the door and noticed that the girls were still screaming, but Coach Sheila was sitting on the floor, so she, thank goodness, wasn't killing them.

Grace hollered in between screams, "Snake, snake."

Jaybird went over to the girls and saw a small snake slithering around. He kicked it with his foot toward the door and it went out.

Intriguing Escapade at Swim Camp

Hally, Maggie, and Bell had Sheila under control. Maggie and Hally were holding her legs so she wouldn't kick them, while Bell had her in a chock hold. The men thought they had her down, so they began untying the girls. They noticed the bruises on the girls' legs and faces. They looked at Sheila and asked why she did that to them, and all she did was spit at them, so Hally went over and punched Coach Sheila on the jaw.

"Now, how does it feel to be punched in the face?" asked Hally after she punched Coach Sheila.

Grace and Silver had big mouths and the other two were sitting still and doing nothing. I just felt like hitting someone, I guess." The coaches wanted to hit Sheila, but knew it wasn't right. They don't have to stoop to her level, although, it made them feel better when Hally punched her.

They heard a noise at the door and in walked an old woman with a monkey, a tiger, a pig, a black cat, and large snake. "Hi, Zeke. Introduce me to your friends," said the lady who looked like she was ninety, if she was a day.

"We came to help. If you tie up the mean woman, my animals can sit with her, so she won't run away," the old lady cackled like a chicken when she said that.

The coaches looked at her group of animals and Jaybird said, "I think that would be a grand idea."

They tied up Coach Sheila to a post like she did to the girls. Miss Izzy put her snake on the floor right beside Shelia. She put the Mikey, the monkey, in her lap. The tiger, pig, and cat sat by her legs. Sheila's face had an expression on it they will never forget as she sat with her animal friends. Sheila just knew her life was over, because she was about to be the animals' supper.

They heard voices outside of the door. Daniel opened it and let the police inside and there were some men with them, who the police introduced as Sheila's brothers. Sheila began crying when she saw her brothers that she hadn't seen in a few years. They probably won't have anything to do with her since she hasn't seen them in so long.

The brothers walked over to their sister, hugged her, and told her they would get her a lawyer, because she would most likely be going to jail unless the lawyer could get her off. Her brothers couldn't believe what she had been doing and thought she needed some sort of punishment. She shouldn't get off with a light sentence with all she had been doing.

The tallest of the policemen walked over to Sheila and said, "Sheila Brown, you are under arrest for child abuse, child endangerment, and kidnapping." Then he quoted her the Miranda Rights.

The policeman hesitated when he untied Sheila because of all the animals that were around her. "Izzy, take you animals home, please."

"Yes Sir, Earl," said Izzy with a huge smile.

The policemen handcuffed Sheila and took her to their police car. The coaches noticed the big tears running down her cheeks.

Chapter Forty-Seven

As Coach Sheila stared out the window of the police car, she began thinking about what she had done, and it didn't look good for her. She saw the other policeman making pictures of the bruises she had put on the girls. If she could go back, she would not have done these things. Her therapist always told her she could change, but she didn't. She couldn't seem to get it out of her system. Her therapist would be disappointed with her, as she should.

She knew when she went to court, there would be many parents who would most likely come to testify about what she did to their children. No, it didn't look good for her and she knew it. She remembers all the girls she had harmed in some way or another. She was sorry for it, but they probably wouldn't take that into consideration, especially since she was still harming kids. The court will see that she has not stopped harming girls, and there was the thing with the boy on the zipline that now has a broken leg because of what Sheila did.

She wanted to talk to her brothers. That would make her feel better. She was glad they were there, so she could talk to them and

Intriguing Escapade at Swim Camp

get a big hug. She knew they loved her and would do what they could for her. She wasn't having much hope for getting away with what she has done.

Her brothers tried their best to raise me, but she didn't always listen to them. She was younger than her brothers and thought she didn't need to do what they said. She will listen to them now. She knew she should have gotten together with them more often, but she was always busy doing her swim thing with the kids, which has not turned out too well for her.

Her dad was getting a little too old and can't remember much anymore. His Dementia is taking over his brain. She was so sad to see him that way that she didn't go see him much. No matter how he was, she should have gone to see him more. He would have liked that. Her brothers always told her to go see him, but she didn't pay much attention to them. She was a bad bad person.

She wanted to make everything right with her brothers and her dad. If she gets out of this, she will go see all of them more often, especially her dad, who always called her his little girl. Now she feels even worse because of her neglect to see her dad and brothers.

Chapter Forty-Eight

The girls had promised to go see Izzy and Rusty before they left camp for home. They asked the coaches to go with them, and they said they would go. The coaches couldn't wait to see where Izzy lives and her animals. The girls had told them a little about her, but they needed to see her in person. The coaches like to meet new people, and this one was special because she has helped the swimmers so much with situations.

They made it to Izzy's cabin and walked upon the front porch with the garlic hanging from the rafters. Before Izzy opened the door, Hank asked the girls a question.

"Why is the garlic hanging up there?" Hank was confused because he had never seen anyone who kept their garlic on the front porch.

"That's easy. It's to keep the vampires away. Apparently, they don't like garlic," smiled Grace who thought it was funny. The others didn't know what to say to that until Hally let curiosity get the better of her.

Intriguing Escapade at Swim Camp

"They have many vampires around here," asked Hally who didn't believe in them, but she would play along.

"She said they may be in the cave," said Lisa who thought this old lady was a hoot.

The door opened and there stood Miss Izzy with that dang ole snake around her neck.

If I need to, I can stay here on the porch if there is not enough room in there for all of us," said Bell, who wasn't about to go inside a house with a large snake, a tiger, a pig, a cat, and monkey named Mikey.

"I can stay with you, so you won't be lonely," Maggie wasn't too keen on going inside either.

"You ladies are so kind, but I have plenty of room. Come on in. I put the animals in the bedroom, so there would be room at the table for all of us," Izzy gave off a huge laugh showing she didn't have any teeth.

They walked inside and was led to sit at the long table. "I want to be a good hostess, so I want to ask how many of you want a cold glass of something to drink. It's sort of hot out there and, since you walked here, you are probably thirsty."

"That would be great, Miss Izzy," said Maggie who volunteered to help her.

"Oh no, ma'am. My guests don't have to work when you come to see me," smiled Izzy with that toothless grin.

Jaybird and Hank took a long swig of their cold drink and got choked. "That's pretty powerful, Miss Izzy," said Jaybird who was still coughing from the long swig he took of his vinegar. The girls and Zeke could have told them about the vinegar, but they wanted them to experience it for themselves.

"Thank you. That is the best vinegar I've ever had. You don't find that too much," Izzy's smile was as big as the moon.

"We noticed your animals. They are so unique. I bet they are good company," said Bell who liked animals.

"Yep. Mikey, that's the monkey helps me with the dishes. The pig's name is Oink. He does nothing to help, and Tigger just plays all day because he's still a little one. My pretty snake is named Sneaky. All of a sudden, the animals must have heard they were being talked about and they all started growling, oinking, or making monkey noises.

"It sounds like the Rainforest Café in here," said Dan who was liking this immensely. He had the makings of a bright smile on his face as he listened to the noises coming from the bedroom.

Intriguing Escapade at Swim Camp

"Well, we don't want to wear out our welcome, so we will be going now," said Hally as everyone got up from the table. They hugged Izzy and told her goodbye.

"If you are ever out this way again, please come visit," said the helpful hostess.

"Bye, Miss Izzy. Thank you so much for your hospitality," they all said together.

Chapter Forty-Nine

They were all at the firepit roasting marshmallows after their meal. It had been a good camp, but it was time to go home the next morning. The competition was the day after they left for home. They needed some rest after all the swimming they had done while here at the camp. They also enjoyed the zipline until it had been broken and the boy broke his leg all because of what Coach Sheila did.

They did have some adventures along the way that they would always remember. They didn't have a clue about Coach Sheila when they first got here. The girls had heard the coaches talking about her secret and they were flabbergasted about the news. They weren't too sure what to do about it but decided saying nothing was better than her finding out they knew.

They loved going to see Miss Izzy. She had helped them when the illegal gambling men was chasing them. They liked it because she had so many strange animals, and she had that garlic hanging on her front porch to chase off vampires. Even if there were such thing as vampires, the girls were not too sure garlic would shoo them away, but she was a nice lady to help them like she did several times.

"Do you remember her shimming up that tall tree like she was a young chick," said Zeke, who was amazed to see the old lady go up a huge tree that fast or go up one at all since she was so old.

"There was Rusty, who volunteered to help us rescue Zeke when the gambling men took him out of the bunkhouse while they were sleeping," said Lisa who had come out of her stupor of her visit to the barn. She had never been tied to a post in an old barn before. None of the kids had ever been tied to anything.

Besides the Coach Sheila debacle and being kidnapped, it was a good camp. The other coaches that came, showed them how to do all four of the strokes efficiently they would need to do at the competition. They helped them so much. They got in the water with us and demonstrated, and then helped the students to do them correctly. They were excited to go to the competition because they felt like they were truly ready for this. They would always remember the adventures they had at the swim camp, and hoped they were able to go there again.

They all walked toward the bus that would take them back to the school, so they could meet their parents to take them home. The coaches told them to get some rest and be ready tomorrow for the competition.

Chapter Fifty

The girls woke from their slumber ready to tackle the competition they had been preparing for at the swim camp the last few days. They packed their gym bags with the needed necessities such as goggles, swim caps, extra swimsuit, and whatever else they might need for the competition. They were not nervous, but they felt confident they had been trained to do the best swim ever. The coaches had prepared them well, and they were there to help them.

They saw their coaches walk through the door to the pool. They were all smiles to see their swimmers ready to do this competition. It made them think of their own competitions when they were young. The coaches couldn't wait for the competition to begin, so they could see how well the girls and boys do. They knew the girls were great swimmers, but sometimes nerves take over.

The four friends went to their coaches and hugged them. They told the coaches they were ready, and they were not nervous at all because they were confident in their strokes. They had taught them well. That made the coaches feel good about what they had

Intriguing Escapade at Swim Camp

accomplished with the girls at the camp. The coaches told them to pay attention to what they were doing and have fun.

The coaches told the girls they would be doing Individual Medley, and they will be doing the relay to obtain more points for the school team. Choose your stroke, ladies.

The moment had come for the competition to begin. Swimmers were shaking their arms and legs getting ready for their swim event. The lady on the microphone said, "We will start with the Individual Medley. Swimmers, take your places."

The girls were lining up, and still they were not nervous. They were having fun, and that made them happy. The coaches were smiling at the girls laughing and having fun. It made them feel good too. The coaches that had helped them, told them they could have fun with the competition. It helps not to be nervous. They were so much better coaches than Coach Sheila.

"Ready, Set, BANG!" went the announcer, and off they went swimming in their lane. Parents were hollering, coaches hollering kick, kick, kick, swimmers' arms stroking, hearts pounding, and blood was pumping as the swimmers did their laps to the best of their ability.

The Individual Medley was over. Swimmers and coaches were waiting patiently for the results to be tallied. Anticipation for the results were running high as they waited and waited. Finally, the microphone lady began giving the results, "We want to thank all the coaches and swimmers here today for the great race we just had. We have the names of the top four places. Number four is Gold Gillygut, number three is Lisa Acre, number two is Silver Gillygut, and number one is Grace Waldon. The girls were going wild as they jumped up and down yelling to the top of their lungs. They were so excited and happy for each other. They were hugging each other and laughing.

The lady came back on the microphone and said she had a special announcement, "Ladies and gentlemen, I have a special announcement. Grace Waldon, would you please come to the stand with the coaches."

Grace was confused and didn't really want to go, but one of her coaches waved at her to come see what they wanted.

"The announcement I have to make is that Grace Waldon has broken her school's record of Individual Medley."

Grace stood with her mouth and eyes wide open. She didn't know what to do or say. They told her she would get a trophy later with her name engraved on it. Her parents, friends, and coaches were jumping up and down laughing.

Grace and her friends were ready to do the relay. With a team of winners such as these girls, they gathered more points than any other relay swimmers in the building.

It had been a great day for Grace and her friends. Their parents took the girls, and the coaches out to eat after the competition was finished. What a day! The four girls who took over the pool today were jubilant.

Epilogue

The four friends walked away from the natatorium with light hearts and smiles on their faces. The swim camp was just what they needed to help them be better swimmers. Of course, they could have done without the adventures, one of which was of Coach Sheila being a mean person, who didn't seem to care about anyone, but she was caught and lost her job.

The girls and Zeke really liked the adventure with Miss Izzy. She was so much fun to be around even if she did have all those animal friends, and man, could she ever shimmy up a tree in record time. They wished they would be that agile when they got to be ninety. She really helped them though when she saved them from the illegal gambling men.

Zeke was fine even after being kidnapped by those same gambling men, but it all worked out well when the police dropped by and took the gambling men with them to the jail.

The coaches, who came to the camp to help, were much better coach than Coach Sheila, who they found out wasn't a very nice person.

Intriguing Escapade at Swim Camp

They heard that Sheila Brown would be going to her trial next month. She will be charged with child endangerment, child abuse, and kidnapping. It didn't look too good for her at all. She would definitely be doing some time.

Everything worked out well for the girls. They all got a trophy, and Grace got an even bigger one, since she broke the school's record for Individual Medley. All the girls, plus Zeke were glad they all did so well, and they made a vow to always help each other and be life-long friends. It truly was an intriguing escapade at swim camp, and one they will never forget.